This book is for my family.

... love consists in a mutual interchange by the two parties. ...

IGNATIUS OF LOYOLA, *Spiritual Exercises* (1533)

WHORES FOR GLORIA

William T. Vollmann was born in Los Angeles in 1959. He attended Deep Springs College and Cornell University, where he graduated *summa cum laude* in comparative literature. In 1982 he crossed into Afghanistan with Islamic commandos, and afterwards lived for several years in San Francisco. Vollmann's books include the novels *You Bright and Risen Angels, The Ice-Shirt, Fathers and Crows,* and *Whores for Gloria* (all available from Penguin); three story collections, *The Rainbow Stories, Thirteen Stories and Thirteen Epitaphs,* and *The Butterfly Stories*; and a work of nonfiction, *An Afghanistan Picture Show*. Vollmann won a 1988 Whiting Award in recognition of his writing achievements and the Shiva Naipaul Memorial Award in 1989. He is currently engaged in writing a series of seven novels exploring the repeated collisions between North American native populations and their colonizers and oppressors; the sixth volume, *The Rifles,* will be published by Viking in February of 1994. William Vollmann lives in California.

"Lucid, lyrical, acrobatically imaginative, William T. Vollmann is one of the few writers around who remind us there are some explorations into the human condition that can best be accomplished through fiction."
—Paul Gediman, *Mirabella*

"A touching, wonderfully uncharacteristic novel. . . . [William Vollmann] is a genuine writer . . . [and] the intricate sympathy he [establishes] among his subjects [is] an essential part of his achievement."
—Eli Gottlieb, *Voice Literary Supplement*

"*Whores for Gloria* is a fascinating narrative attack. . . . Vollmann writes with deceptive simplicity—very talented and daring—[and] he is part of an important new movement in American fiction, vital and brutally contemporary."
—Vince Passaro, *New York Newsday*

WHORES FOR GLORIA

William T. Vollmann

Penguin Books

PENGUIN BOOKS
Published by the Penguin Group
Penguin Books USA Inc., 375 Hudson Street, New York, New York 10014, U.S.A.
Penguin Books Ltd, 27 Wrights Lane, London W8 5TZ, England
Penguin Books Australia Ltd, Ringwood, Victoria, Australia
Penguin Books Canada Ltd, 10 Alcorn Avenue, Toronto, Ontario, Canada M4V 3B2
Penguin Books (N.Z.) Ltd, 182-190 Wairau Road, Auckland 10, New Zealand

Penguin Books Ltd, Registered Offices: Harmondsworth, Middlesex, England

First published in Great Britain by Pan Books Ltd, 1991
First published in the United States of America by Pantheon Books,
a division of Random House, Inc., 1992
Reprinted by arrangement with Pantheon Books
Published in Penguin Books 1994

10 9 8 7 6 5 4 3 2

THE LIBRARY OF CONGRESS HAS CATALOGUED THE HARDCOVER AS FOLLOWS:
Vollmann, William T.
Whores for Gloria/William T. Vollmann.
p. cm.
ISBN 0-679-40432-6 (hc.)
ISBN 0 14 02.3157 9 (pbk.)
I. Title.
PS3572.0395W4 1992
813'.54—dc20   91–52626

Printed in the United States of America

The Album

We all know the story of the whore who, finding her China white to be less and less reliable a friend no matter how much of it she injected into her arm, recalled in desperation the phrase "shooting the shit", and so filled the needle with her own watery excrement and pumped it in, producing magnificent abscesses. Less well known is the tale of the man who decided to kill himself by swallowing his athlete's foot medicine. Loving Gloria, he died in inconceivable agony. When they collected a sample of his urine, it melted the plastic cup. — *That*, it is safe to say, is despair. More obscure still, because fictitious, is the following. All of the whore's-tales herein, however, are real.

Jimmy

Once upon a time when Laredo the blonde police decoy was working on a drug bust she watched a man speaking into a pay phone; and as it got dark the sky filled with clouds like rushing bombs and Laredo stood on the corner of Jones and Sutter picking at wrinkles in her skirt and acting like a whore and trolling for whores and pimps and johns and dealers and whatever else might come her way and the man kept talking into the pay phone and the longer he talked the less notice Laredo took of him because her prey usually looked both ways and placed the call and spoke for five seconds and then walked away with rapid steps glaring around with nervous bloodshot eyes but this man kept talking and talking and holding the receiver tight in both hands; once upon a time Laredo leaned up against the fire hydrant crossing her legs and waiting for some stupe to offer her money so she could write him a ticket; and old people hobbled home to their hotels to double-lock their half-rotten doors for the night and it got darker and darker and the whores came out and sat on the hoods of old station wagons and Laredo spied on them with the all-seeing eyes of a snorkeler; and behind a dark curtain inside a dented van across the street her partner Leroy, who was new, sipped at his Orange Crush and spotted her like a good boy. The street was full of night-sharks. It was alarming at first for Leroy to see their faces so close in the field of his binoculars, thinking that surely they must see him, and when the faces scowled directly at him and came closer, closer like rushing sinister meteors he flinched, *knowing* then that *surely* they must be coming at him, but at the last moment the faces flicked to the side. Light ran upon the moving cars like quicksilver. A man in a grey jacket swung his arms bitterly. A man in a raincoat reached into his pocket and pulled out something twisted up in a toilet paper and another man looked both ways and gave him twenty dollars for it. A man was talking on the pay phone as he had been doing for a good quarter-hour; Leroy, who could read lips, focused on him every now and then and saw that he was saying Gloria and Gloria and Gloria. *He* did not know, evidently, but Leroy knew that the fat lady with the dirty-blonde hair knew because she had been there when Laredo got out of the van hours ago saying wow Leroy this is *great*! no one can see past the front seat!—and the fat lady was still there and she paced back and forth on the corner and men came by and gave her little pieces of paper which she tucked away into her coat pocket and she kept looking straight at Leroy and walked up to the van and never looked away from Leroy and then turned and walked away.—Is the light glinting on my binoculars? Leroy asked himself. But surely Laredo would have told me.—So he sat there unhappily.—A man in a blue cap stood on the corner; he smiled and winked at Leroy. Two young women stood laughing and leaning against a lamppost; then they suddenly became serious and directed their gaze straight at Leroy.—Did they all see him? Did any of them see him? He would never know. With his binoculars he was like a young bird that has just learned to fly, but does not trust its wings. The new power that the binoculars had given him was not something that he could trust.—Yet the girls did not move away or shield their faces from him, and soon they were looking in other directions; soon a car honked and pulled over and one of the girls smiled and smoothed her skirt and got in. An aged blonde clopped by like a horse as she inhaled on her cigarette, and her face was lined with grief.—Laredo shifted her aching feet, wishing that the night would end although she was well aware that by the laws of astronomy the night would not end till morning; neither, it

3

seemed, would the drunk on the pay phone. Well fuck it *she* could take it because in two more weeks she and her husband would be going on vacation, this year to Hawaii to rent a condo on the Kona coast where there were many restaurants with big open windows through which at night the ocean was black and white and green, roaring in with its boiled-snake smell right below the railing where you sat by candlelight trying to make out the menu while the other patrons laughed loudly and threw cigarette butts out to sea, and even after the sea killed their glow you could still see them there in the water, so white and clean-looking. Every morning Laredo's husband went surfing and Laredo watched him with warm and sleepy smiles in between nibbling reads at her paperback and then commenced the real business of the day by fitting on her rented mask and tube and flippers and tightening the straps just so and then gathering everything in her arms like an offering as she began to wade into the warm water, feeling cautiously with her toes for sharp coral and enjoying the hot sun on her back and stepping out deeper and deeper until the waves slopped gently at her belly and she put the mask around her neck and popped on her flippers one by one and took a deep breath and slid the mask down onto her face and bit hard on the breathing tube and stretched out her arms and raised her legs and put her head under, and for a second her face felt cold and funny around the edges of her mask and then there was the sea-world again, of which she was the Empress, ruling proudly over the coral hills, which were not unlike the cactus-studded sandhills of the American southwest—for each coral-bush and coral-flower, no matter how many layers of delicacy it may possess, can be seen through to hardness; and the red sea-urchins bristled their spines like yuccas, and the little pale ones were like chollas:— across this desertscape (which was comprised of mountains in miniature, for no coral hill was more than two or three feet high, and Laredo floated in touching distance of them all) swam hundreds of brightly colored fish: long thin green

4

ones, with red stripes and blue fins; round yellow fish like swirling eucalyptus leaves; great silvery fish whose cool bellies she could have stroked, had she wanted to, with her quick fingers; tiny blue fish with black bandit-masks, and ever so many more. They swam in schools, or in cross-currents; they seemed entirely unaware of Laredo as she hung there with her face in the water like a drowned corpse, watching them through her mask-window, on the inner pane of which crawled the droplets of her tears (but actually they were only sea water), and Laredo, being a policewoman, believed that if she floated there long enough she would know everything about them, and she drifted along in the warm waves, while just outside this world the sun warmed her back and tanned it more and more perfectly right through the slick salt seadrops; and Laredo flew over coral canyons in which the fishes unheedingly flurried; but presently the valleys grew deeper; the bottom began to drop away, and the coral became grey and lifeless, so that had Laredo looked the merest yard ahead (which she did not do) she would have seen a rich blue wall of shadow where the ocean was a hundred feet deep. That was where the damned drunk *still* stood, talking and talking into the pay phone as if he had a direct line to the Whore of Wisdom, while the cars crawled slowly down the street with glowing red eyes and a cold wind turned the pages of newspapers on the sidewalk (for the air was eagerly reading the news), and the strap of Laredo's handbag (in which she kept her little back-up revolver) dug into her shoulder as she stood with bored patience watching the man leaning forward inside the phone booth as if that would somehow diminish the distance between him and the person he was talking to, and the soft bulk of the yellow pages padded his thighs;— once upon a time a man made a phone call, and the man was crying. Only Laredo and Leroy could see that he was crying. The person to whom he was talking would never have known it. His voice was very low and gentle and even. His voice was patient and tender. The phone did not shake his hands.

Once upon a time a man made a phone call.—What else did the doctor say? the man asked gently.—Gloria? Gloria, what did the doctor say? Are you crying, Gloria? If I can buy you a plane ticket tonight will you come tonight? Yes, Gloria, you can take a taxi cab to the airport, can't you? Gloria? Gloria? I got some money. I can give you some money.—So is my little baby kicking inside you? Is it a girl or a boy? I didn't forget about you. I never forgot about you, Gloria. I never stopped thinking about you. Are you going to have my baby? I got lots of money now. I can take care of you, Gloria. When are you going to get the abortion? Are you smoking a lot of cigarettes? Gloria? Gloria, are you still there? How's it goin', Gloria? Gloria, I'll be waitin' for you.

The man hung up at last, very carefully and gently, as if the weight of the receiver inside the cradle might break something inside the woman. Then he turned the yellow pages with a frown and scratched the stubble on his cheeks and finally dialled another number.—Yeah he said I want to make reservations on the night plane tomorrow for Gloria Evans that's right from L.A. OK that's right OK ten o'clock you said? Whatever's cheapest.—*How* much? Eighty bucks? You're fucking kidding.—What do you mean watch my language just find something cheaper . . . that's the *best* you can do? I heard that one before. Hey babe you got a beautiful voice what's your name how old are you?—Why you sweet young thing, you're old enough to be my mother so just pretend you're my mother; think of me and help me out. Can you give me a discount; can I jerk off to you? *Wow*, you're NICE; you didn't even hang up on me! All right now babe I'm counting on you to make sure Gloria's on that plane because she can't take care of herself she needs help in everything she does so you take care of her then you take

6

care of me. Let's get together.—Aw, come on! Hey, I'm clean—you just ask *any* whore in the Tenderloin! I've never cheated on *any* one of my women even when I was goin' out with all three of 'em at the same time.

The man laughed. He hung up. He winked at Laredo and sauntered off whistling. But Laredo was no fool. She knew that the pay phone had been broken for weeks. And she knew that the man was still crying.

3

Decisions, decisions

When everything—*EVERYTHING*—about life makes you want to grin, and it just gets sunnier and funnier until after a while you can only see the teeth in the smiles and then you feel . . . —well, not "on the edge", exactly, for the world has no edge; but as if you have always been *over* the edge, and the smiling and laughing is a sort of spastic reflex like crying or retching (really, it's all the same);—when you drink red wine in a cup and try to categorize the geometry of the gleam-patterns you see on the liquid's surface—and you may find, my friends, that you can almost do it: you agree with yourself upon the existence of a light-shape like the outline of a hemisphere drawn in concave at the equator; but another sip and it changes to a gleam-ring all around the rim of the wine circle; and another and it is reddish-black everywhere with the unsteady image of your face in it, your skin redder and your mouth blacker than the wine, and another and you see white specks swimming in the cup: they are not reflections at all, but bits of grease or rice or cereal, or maybe cheek-cells that got washed out of your mouth (the age-old question: is the imperfection, the filth, in you or in the glass?);—but then your attention is diverted forever by the ugly purple stain around the edge of the cup where your lips have been; when everything is so confusing that you can never be sure whether or not your whore is a woman until she pulls her underpants down; when nothing is clear, and whore-chasing is a merry-go-round of death (if you don't catch a disease that will kill you, why, you will go around again, not because you want to die but because until you do everything remains unclear); when you get drunken crushes on women whose drunken mothers used to try to stab them; when the names of streets are like Nabokov's wearisome cleverness; when only the pretty shapes of women have integrity and when you close your eyes still see them leaning and crossing their legs and milking their tits at you, THEN you may on occasion like Jimmy find yourself looking down a long black block, down the tunnels of infinity to a streetlamp, a corner and a woman's waiting silhouette.—Or else like Jimmy you may have another drink.

The Black Rose

On one of those days when at two in the afternoon it was still morning because Jimmy had woken up with the dry heaves and the thought of a beer almost gave him the wet heaves, so he was sitting in the Black Rose drinking watery orange juice and nasty tomato juice and a whore came up to ask him for a quarter to do her laundry and it was more of an effort to get rid of her than to give her the quarter and the electronic sign-strip over the video screen said CECILY—CECILY—CECILY and Cecily stood behind the bar and said Hey, baby to Jimmy softly when he came in and he was not sure whether he had been there a long time or whether he had just gotten there but Cecily was looking so chubby and adorable in her sweater (but Jimmy knew that Cecily was a man) and Cecily trudged back and forth pouring bucketfuls of crushed ice into the beer cooler and men in cowboy hats sat in the back shadows nodding to the country music while outside the sunshine was so hot and bright that the pissy reek of Jones Street gave Jimmy ONE (1), TWO (2), THREE (3) dry heaves—on one of those early afternoon mornings, then, Jimmy decided to get drunk—not just drunk enough to enjoy life (here he grinned, and Cecily smiled back), not just drunk

enough to fuck Cecily for instance up the ass without a
rubber, not just drunk enough to hear bees buzzing round
his ears and wake up in another bad place he'd never seen
before with crushed bugs on the walls and men maybe standing over him looking down at him with their teeth drawn
away from their lips, and puke cold and sticky all over his
face again, puke being the concretization of Jimmy's disgust
with Jimmy whose eyes would be burning and throat burning
and stomach squirming like a guilty squid and every muscle
aching, and the dry heaves inside him just like heartbeats,
just like yesterday;—no, he wanted to be drunk enough to
scientifically establish the existence of the whores that he
could see all around him. (Jimmy had always liked whores.)
So he started drinking. This kind of drunkenness required
more alcohol than the buzzing kind; but the alcohol must be
spaced out. He had his first Budweiser and he had his
second. He had his first Corona with a lemon slice and that
was all for the Coronas because they were more expensive;
maybe that was why Cecily chose them when he said buy
you a drink Cess?—What was her markup? Ten twenty thirty
percent. And he tipped her, too. Jimmy would sooner go
without than leave no tip. His friend Code Six who knew all
the jokes thought Jimmy was soft that way but Jimmy always
said they have to make a living too and if I tip them they'll
look out for me.—They'll look out for you, all right, said
Code Six. You and your wallet. If your wallet's got pimples
they'll pop it for you.—You sure you don't want another
Corona, baby? said Cecily.—Thanks anyhow, said Jimmy.
You know how it is when you're hungover. That lemon kind
of set your teeth on edge.—If Jimmy had been anyone else
Cecily might have said aw come on I'll give it to you without
the lemon but Cecily never pushed Jimmy because he was
generous. He was not her best customer but he was a good
one.—He had a shot of whiskey and his third Budweiser.
Once when Cecily wasn't working she bought Jimmy another
shot of whiskey, but he was not sure whether that was this

time or last time; anyhow, here was the shot sitting in front
of him on a new napkin, and he didn't see any of his money
on the bar anymore so he must not have paid for it. More
beautiful than the gleam of quarters on the bar was the feeling
that there was something else that he would remember later,
and more beautiful than that was the way Cecily took care
of him, whisking away his napkin every time he crumpled it
and rushing him a fresh one, or sweeping away his crumbs,
or lighting his cigarette for him. Energy came into him with
each beer, more energy each time so that everything seemed
happier and happier, more and more energy leaping inside
him like the bad bald men leaping into other bars with their
Bomber T-shirts to make everyone cheer.

These were days when my heart was volcanic (said Poe)
As the scoriac rivers that roll—
As the lavas that restlessly roll
Their sulphurous currents down Yaanek,
In the ultimate climes of the Pole—
That groan as they roll down Mount Yaanek,
In the realms of the Boreal Pole. *

Now Jimmy was very happy although for a moment he
thought that he had betrayed someone and he fell in love
with Kelly, whose beautiful black face did not look like a
man's except outside the bar (bars are dim for a reason), and
Jimmy fell in love with Cecily because he was sweet to Jimmy
and promised that he would make Jimmy up, but Regina,
who was now the barmaid, was so lovely that he wanted to
kiss her black face, and she kissed his hand; however, fat
Puerto Rican Phyllis the heroin bitch, who might *really* have
been a woman, came and sat between Jimmy and Regina and
squeezed their dicks and put her heavy muscular arms around
them both and gave them her breasts to squeeze and picked

---

* "Ulalume" (1847).

11

Jimmy's pocket. The light was very red and warm; the girls were beautiful, and everything was beautiful until later when the girls got anxious and started demanding their tips.

Nicole

The next thing Jimmy knew, he was on the street and it was dark and he was whore-hunting. He saw women dancing on the sidewalk; he was sure that they offered both acute and obtuse triangles; but they would not go to his hotel and he did not want to go to theirs because he did not like to feel trapped at the same time that he felt dizzy.—How fine the moonlight was, though! It made him retch.—He saw a whore leaning against the side of a reflective building, waggling her skinny knees although her high heels and her butt did not move and her head was cocked against her shoulder so that she could watch men out of the corner of her stupid little eyes. She said doll you want a date? and Jimmy said thank *you* for the offer but tell you the truth I'm looking for my friend Gloria you know the one with the big tits?—Oh that's just an *excuse*! sneered the whore, at which Jimmy cocked his head very wisely and said I never excuse myself except when I burp. Do you ever burp? Gloria doesn't.—Oh Christ, said the whore, who was as slender and unwholesome looking as a snake, and she stalked around the corner, heels clacking angrily.—Next he had several offers from a pimp who said he *knew* Jimmy would be satisfied, so Jimmy looked as dumb as he could and said wow pal sounds like a good one and you'll never believe this but I left all my money back at my hotel.—Don'tcha even have twenty on ya? said the pimp.— Jimmy said don't I wish but God's truth is I got one hundred two hundred dollars back home in fact I got *lots* of money in fact I think I may even be a *millionaire*, so bring her by pal I only live two hours away from here what do you say?—

When the pimp heard that, he didn't even bother to answer. He crossed the street, shaking his head, and Jimmy stood leaning up against a wall and laughing inside himself with snotty little gurgles like a bottle of Scotch pouring down the toilet. Finally he found a whore who would go with him. He looked around to make sure that the pimp wasn't watching and showed her forty dollars. Her name was Nicole, and she looked rather more than young, twenty-five maybe and strung-out, but not sharp and hard like a piece of broken glass, only used up like a dirty eraser, so he figured she would be OK with her lank hair curling around her ears and her ear-rings of white plastic pearls, so he said Well come on and Nicole looked at him tiredly with her skin stretched dry and tight across her forehead and Jimmy said Nicole your blue eyeliner's smeared you should fix it if you want to stay beautiful and Nicole rubbed her forehead and said she had a headache. He said well come *on* baby come with me then you can buy yourself a painkiller.

I don't usually go to the man's place, Nicole said. You promise you won't hurt me?

I promise, Jimmy said. If I wanted to hurt you, he explained to her very logically, you couldn't get away from me anyway.

That's not true, said Nicole. I could kill you easy.

Well see, said Jimmy grandly, you have nothing to worry about. You can kill me easy, so why be nervous?

He took her up the street and she kept asking how far it was. Three more blocks, said Jimmy. The light glowed in her hair.

The first thing she asked to do was use the bathroom. He heard her shit. I suppose she must be nervous, he said to himself. Jimmy had once been a reader, so he knew how in Auschwitz or Treblinka there was a ramp leading up to the gas chambers called the Road to Heaven where all the women had to wait naked and squatting while the men were finished being gassed (they went first because they did not need to have their hair cut off for the submarine crews), and while

13

the sheared women waited they usually emptied their bowels and the guards laughed and laughed like hooded pimps in an alley and now history repeated itself as Jimmy stood nipping on a fresh beer and waiting for Nicole to complete the preparations for her little ordeal. Well, he said to himself, *I can't help it if she's nervous. She's got a job to do.*

Silently he said Gloria, are you still there? Gloria?

When Nicole came into the kitchen she was naked except for her red shirt.—You want a half-and-half? she said.

Sure, Jimmy said.

Will you *take care of me* first? she said smiling; her face glowed, she seemed so sweet like Gloria.

Sure I will, he said, what do you want me to do? (He thought she meant for him to jerk her off or otherwise *affect* her. He sometimes liked to fool himself.)

Will you pay me first? Nicole said patiently.

Oh fine, Jimmy said. He got the forty dollars out of his wallet and gave it to her.

Then Nicole sat down on the chair in the kitchen and took his penis in her hand and he saw how her arms were discolored everywhere with abscesses and needle tracks and he leaned forward a little so that Nicole could put his penis into her mouth and she began to suck at it smoothly, rapidly and Jimmy looked down at the top of her head and wondered if her eyes were open or closed and then he looked at the wall and watched a cockroach crawling down between the gas pipe and the sink, and he listened to the noises that her lips made sucking his penis, and he listened to the loud ticking of her cheap plastic watch. Jimmy was not thinking about anything in particular, but his penis began to get hard right away. As soon as it was entirely stiff like some dead thing, she took it out of her mouth and rolled a rubber onto it with her lined and grimy hands.—Now take your shirt off, Jimmy said.—He stepped back from her and dropped his clothes to the floor. Nicole sat wearily on the chair, rubbing her forehead. When she pulled her shirt over her head he saw that she had a cast on her left wrist. Her breasts were big and sad like owls' eyes.

You want my coat for a pillow? said Jimmy.

Nicole shook her head.

All right then, he said, get down on the floor.

The kitchen floor was black with dirt. Nicole lay down on it and raised her legs to make her cunt so nice and tight for him, and Jimmy stood over her watching the groping of those legs, which were speckled with boils and lesions, until her left ankle came to rest on the chair that she had sat on, while the sole of her right foot had to be content with bracing itself against Jimmy's refrigerator. Her breasts lay limp on her belly, as round as the faces or polished brass pendulums of clocks. Jimmy stood enjoying her for another moment, liking the way she looked as she lay there between the refrigerator and the wall, brown-skinned and almost pretty, with a white plastic cross between her tits.

Are you Catholic? he said.

Yes, Nicole said.

Jimmy strode around naked except for his socks, inspecting her cunt like an emperor. This was the best part. Nicole gazed up at him and pulled the lips of her slit taut and up to show him the ragged pear of pinkness inside, and her cunt-lips glistened under the kitchen lights with the brightness of metal foil. —Your pussy is just like a flower*, Jimmy complimented her; all the same he did not want to get his face too close to it. He got down on his knees; he leaned his weight on his arms as if he were doing push-ups (for Jimmy was always a gentleman who would not hurt a woman with his weight); then he stuck his penis into her. She had told him that he was her first date of the night, but her cunt seemed to be full of something viscous like come or corn syrup.

---

* "I still remember the effect I produced on a small group of Gala tribesmen massed around a man in black clothes," wrote Vittorio Mussolini. "I dropped an aerial torpedo right in the center and the group opened up like a flowering rose. It was most entertaining."

Maybe it was just the lubricant she used. Anyhow, it stank. She had great black spots on her thighs that might have been moles or more probably the subcutaneous hemorrhages of Kaposi's syndrome as Jimmy well knew from his profoundly intellectual studies. Every time he thrust into her she grunted. He could not tell whether this was because he hurt her or because she did it to excite him and so get it over with faster. He did not feel that she hated him and her body was trying to expel him; more probably she just endured him and trusted to the frictionlessness of the corn syrup or whatever it was to protect her from being hurt by his thrusts (in direct proportion as *his* sensation was diminished), but the corn syrup did not much work anymore to soothe that red raw-rubbed meat between her legs, so Nicole just tried not to think about what was happening and grunted at Jimmy's every painful thrust and bit her lips whenever he grazed an ovary. She gripped his balls tightly all the time so that the rubber wouldn't slip; she dug her fingernails into his balls, either by mistake or to make him come. But after thirty seconds Jimmy knew that he wasn't going to be able to come. Maybe if she'd just sucked him off he could have done it, but what with the rubber and the stuff in her cunt he couldn't feel much. Jimmy fucked and fucked until he got bored and then told her that he was done. — Call me, he said politely. — Later his prick started to itch, and he worried about disease.

The harvest

I wonder if she gave me something, he said to himself. He could not stop thinking about it. He got a black pimple on his penis, and his balls ached. — *But I used a rubber!* he said in despair. Of course, she did suck me before she put it on.

The next day he said to himself, I definitely have something.

16

The lecture

At the clinic all the chairs faced the same direction, as if the venereally contaminated were an expectant movie audience instead of what they were. The chairs were bolted to the floor. Jimmy sat scratching his greyish chin-stubble and reading the notices on the walls and wondering if he could duck into the bathroom for just a minute to drink a beer because the place dispirited him, but he decided that that would not be a good idea and anyway he did not have a beer with him. Finally they called his number, and a woman led him into a little room with a desk and a stool.

What are you here for? said the woman.

I had sex with a prostitute on Friday night and I think she gave me something, Jimmy said.

When did you say you had sex with the prostitute? the woman said.

Friday night.

That would be the 26th, she said, looking at the wall calendar.—All right, let's see a driver's license.

Let's see your penis, said the doctor sternly.

Jimmy pointed out to the doctor the black pimple, but the doctor laughed and ripped it off his penis with a gloved hand so that his penis bled.—That's only a zit, said the doctor. But I tell you, anyone who'd go to a prostitute ought to have his head examined. I think you're all right. Follow the yellow line; they'll give you a blood test for syphilis.

Gloria

The next day Jimmy breakfasted on aspirin and ice cream. He felt pretty down. Well James he said to himself it's time to turn over a new leaf and really work at thinking about Gloria and remember how she appeared to me and ask of her that she give me her love and never again go for diseased imitations like that draggly old Nicole bitch who had nothing in common with Gloria and cheated me anyhow by never moving underneath me so I might as well have been fucking a pork chop and I know in my heart that *that's* something that Gloria would never have done, bless her heart. And Jimmy remembered how sadly Nicole had sat naked in his kitchen chair, with her hands beneath her sagging ass, and her head slumped back against the wall. Her mouth curved downward in her face, and her cunt-lips hung loosely apart like wilting lettuce.—But he also knew that every bit of it was his fault. Once he was on top of Nicole he had let his mind wander; he had not been thinking about Gloria. And the other whore had been right: he *had* just been using Gloria as an excuse—which come to think of it was like taking her name in vain. And what had he been doing in the Black Rose playing around with Regina and Cess? He admitted that he hadn't been taking Gloria very seriously. But Gloria is all I have, he said. OK then he said from now until the whole Tenderloin falls down in the next earthquake I'm going to hold onto Gloria and well I guess I'm repeating myself but I do usually think about her.

Gloria

The truth is that Jimmy tried *never* to stop thinking of Gloria. Even when he bent women over as they spread the cheeks of their buttocks apart so that he could fuck them up their assholes which bulged like the ends of sausage-casings, he was thinking of Gloria.

Gloria

OK he said all those whores out there are for me but they also each have something to give to Gloria if I can just find out what that is and help Gloria along like a splash of light on the ocean and everything moving and rocking and shining in the sun so God help me now because Gloria is the great sea those whore-fish swim in; God help me to give up food so I can spend more of my SSI checks on whores and find what I need to find and God let Gloria grow right with me because I sure don't want to die alone.

The Black Rose

It was loud the next night and the bargirls were beautiful and the bottles were redly back-lit. There were often three bottles of a kind, with the one in use having a tube and stopper like a laboratory flask, so Jimmy felt that he was in a loud laboratory of happiness, where the right combination of reagents would yield gold. Getting warmed up was what he called it. Starting now and for the rest of his life he was going to work at *seeing* Gloria and *remembering* her, and in this special place he became more and more certain that he could do it as long as he did not get ahead of himself and forfeit his desire through rashness or thoughtlessness. — Outside, a woman eating pizza said howdy, but he didn't like her. He went back in and had a beer and a beer. In his mind he saw a newspaper headline:

SECRET OF SOCIAL SUCCESS

Whores Have Done Wonders For My Confidence, Says Leading Alcoholic.

Cecily smiled at him and said don't be so down Jimmy; have another beer.

Korea

On Geary and Hyde he met a black whore named Korea who got on his nerves with all her acting out and acting up but Korea really liked him as it seemed because she was strung out on speed and so she was sweet and serious with Jimmy (whores and undertakers are the only eternal optimists); and she said I *want* you I *need* you 'cause I'm a refugee from Korea so won't you come with me and Jimmy said baby maybe later and Korea said *no* we got to do it *now* 'cause at ten o'clock I got to be checked in at Saint Anthony's or else they'll be sending me back to Africa with all the other black, black people, but don't worry for yourself Jimmy babe 'cause you're so white that heaven's gonna come for you and if I'm good and get to know you and keep tricking for Christ I know you'll let me stay too and not be a refugee from Germany anymore 'cause my name is Berlin; and Jimmy said I thought your name was Korea and Korea screamed now I can see you looking at me with those eyes of death.

Jimmy said eyes or no eyes what's your godamned name I like to know the name of the lady I'm talking to.

Korea said I can call myself any name you want so what do *you* want to call me?

I might call you Gloria, Jimmy said.

Well Jimmy how did you know that Gloria is my name it's actually my real name 'cause I'm a refugee from GLORY. It happened a long time ago when there was juice from pears and peaches in my veins and I used to be able to dance so high you couldn't see me from the steeple of the highest church.

Jimmy said no no no you're not Gloria; Jimmy cried.

In Defense of women

Now Jimmy walked back to Post Street and right to Larkin and left down to Turk Street where it was so hard to escape from pink neon curves and left again for four or five long dark blocks to the place where you could buy marital aids and Big John dolls with rubber mouths to suck you off and other dildoes; in this establishment devoted to increasing the general ecstasy and private well-being the boys were playing video strip poker with films of women who kissed their hands to you from behind the blue screen and talked in low scratchy voices like transvestites; you put in a quarter and then if you won the hand you got to watch the woman of your choice take her shoes off and then it was time to INSERT QUARTER again; if you lost the hand you didn't even get to see that much. — That's how the bitches are in real life too, said a fat boy who had lost and lost, but Jimmy said boy don't ever say that because women need money to stay beautiful for you and that's why I say to you boy never begrudge what you give a woman because you'll see it compounding interest in her eyes and breasts and she will glow for you like you never thought she could and the boy said aw go jerk off you old wino and Jimmy who was still strong grabbed the boy by his neck and lifted him off the floor an inch or so and told him sonny do you want me to pop your eyes out with two fingers or punch you in the nose bone so it smashes up into your brain, if you have a brain that is, or should I chop you on the upper lip and knock your teeth out? I bet you didn't know there's a lot of nerves real close to the skin right there. — Aw right I'm sorry sorry *sorry* choked the boy who was sweating like a pig, and Jimmy let go of his neck and watched him drop that inch back to the floor and as he was walking away he pretended not to hear the boy say you crazy fucking wino.

Remembering the fire

Later that night Jimmy say a leggy blonde who reminded
him a little of Gloria and he got a semi just looking at her
so when he got to the corner he said how's it going? but the
blonde just clopped by him and crossed the street. For a
minute Jimmy was a little down, but he said to himself that
girl was no lady; Gloria would never have done that. (And
he closed his eyes and said Gloria? Gloria, am I remembering
you better than last night?) Then he spied a cute one with a
plump and bouncy butt and he said Gloria if this is the one
tonight I'm asking you to move her to move me and he
followed that bouncing butt for three blocks where the fire
engines were going with screaming sirens and he remembered a night two or three years ago when even after midnight
it was as balmy as Florida and inside all the rat-trap apart-
ments it was too hot to sleep so that at three in the morning
all the whores and pimps stood outside in their shirt sleeves
and everyone was enjoying the weather and whores sat on
the hoods of old cars smoking cigarettes and enjoying the
breeze that went up their miniskirts and cooled off their
smoking pussies and all the windows were thrown wide open
in the hotels but the buildings seemed anyway to be exhaling
steam and sweat from every crack in their stucco or grimy
brickwork and the whores hiked up their dresses even higher
because it was so hot and the whores smiled like tropical
orange juice girls and the whores giggled like little girls
staying up past their bedtime and the moon was full and to
top things off a big fire broke out in a building on Eddy
Street so there was something to watch and until the fire
engines put it out everyone had a fine time. — *This* whore
must not have been there, for she had no party spirit. She
kept walking and walking very briskly although she must have
noticed that Jimmy was following her, so Jimmy called out
hey babe oh *baby* you are *gorgeous* but don't you remember

the fire last fall when we were all so happy well now you're spoiling it for all of us by turning the cold cold shoulder and freezing the fire in my heart even though I've been following you for way over an hour and that's *more* than sixty minutes so what are you afraid of doll *I* got money now come to Daddy, but the whore never looked back, and Jimmy smacked his fist into his palm thinking that bitch is no different than a tampon they're both stuck up cunts and Gloria would never have tolerated her in our home for half a second and he started thinking about giving up and ducking into the 441 Club for a beer and a round of liars' dice with the barmaid when he saw the most beautiful black whore smiling at him on the corner and then he knew that the evening would be a success.

Melissa

You want some company? asked Melissa and Jimmy said I sure do and Melissa said walk with me then and tell me how much you have to spend and Jimmy said I have forty and Melissa was happy with that which made Jimmy happy and Melissa said what do you want me to do with you and Jimmy said I want you to tell me happy stories about when you were a little girl and I'll just kind of sit down and *watch* you and *listen* to you and Melissa said OK honey you follow a little behind me I'm going to cross the street and go into that white building just beside the store, so Jimmy ambled half a block behind her as if he had nothing to do with her at all and a black-and-white police car cruised beside him for a moment but Jimmy never looked at it and finally the police car gave up and drove away and Jimmy watched Melissa's ass twisting and turning in the tight skirt ahead of him and he felt the thrill because he had caught her and she was going to do just what he wanted.

24

Melissa held the grating open for him. The lobby was old-style marble, but as soon as they went upstairs everything was dark and shabby and stinking. Melissa took him around the corner for a minute and stood thinking and then led Jimmy to the elevator. Jimmy's dick was hard. They went down together in the little steel cage, neither saying a thing because they both had exactly what they wanted, and then the cage stopped and they were in the basement. Melissa led him into the laundry room.—Close the door, said Jimmy, but Melissa wouldn't because she was afraid of him.

You remind me of Gloria, said Jimmy.—Who's Gloria? said Melissa.—Oh she used to live around here, Jimmy lied; she moved about three weeks ago. Have you seen her?—No, Melissa said. I've never seen her.

I guess the first thing I wanna do, said Melissa in her low breathy voice, is ask you to tell me exactly what kind of stories you want me to tell.

Tell me some happy stories about when you were a girl.

Oh, happy stories? OK. All right.

One of the happiest things I guess I can remember from being a young child was my first train ride, said Melissa. Most people say they can't remember too much before the age of four or five. I remember clearly when I was three years old taking a train ride to Louisiana to visit my father's grandmother, who was dying. It was the wintertime, I remember, 'cause there was a lot of snow falling when we went through the Colorado mountains there. And I remember having the conductor come through the train in the early morning, saying: *First call for breakfast in the dining car! First call for breakfast in the dining car!* and everybody was bustling around to get to the dining car to eat breakfast. A few mornings we actually had breakfast in the dining car, and it was exciting, being a small child. I remember getting off at the stops along the way. In New Mexico I remember pretty well seeing the Indian jewelry, the stuff you see now, silver and turquoise stuff. And then on through to Texas and finally

Louisiana where I do remember going to New Orleans as a child. One of the things that sticks out in my memory—actually it wasn't happy at all but it sticks out in my memory—was the separate bathrooms for black and white people down there. I remember asking my mother what was colored. That was over twenty years ago now.

Another happy story—I guess I didn't finish that one but anyway it was a memory—was of Christmas time as a young child. The first part of Christmas usually started with going to pick out a huge Christmas tree in the wee morning hours at this supermarket called the Co-op where we used to get our Christmas tree every year, and everybody was frantically out there, dressed up in their heavy clothes—topcoat and boots, maybe, and a hat—scrumming around looked for these Christmas trees. I remember the smell of it still. Then finally by daylight we'd finally find something that was suitable, and I remember dragging it to the car and taking it home and later trimming it. It was just the three of us, though—me, my mom and my dad. Pretty soon that tree started to die, and by Christmas time it was completely dead with needles all over the floor and my mother screaming and vacuuming them up. Anyway, that was the start of the Christmas season. Then I guess the middle part of it was taken up with school things. Learning songs for the Christmas show we'd put on for the parents. Learning some old tacky Christmas carol to sing, everyone's voice singing so ugly and everyone saying that sounds so beautiful.—Melissa laughed in disgust.—And then finally getting all dressed up and on Christmas morning singing it for the parents. And another part of that was towards the end kind of getting antsy, wondering what Santa was going to bring. To this day I think I was the oldest person ever to believe in Santa Claus. I remember when I was eight being told by my mother that there was no Santa and just breaking down in tears and stuff 'cause I didn't want to hear it. 'Cause just a year and a half or so before she'd

26

spank me for trying to tell *her* that I'd heard there was no Santa. Crazy woman. OK, enough about that.

What other happy stories? Let's see, said Melissa as the lights glared brightly down and washing machines hissed and the big pipe hissed beside her, I guess, going shopping with my mom downtown on Saturday afternoons and finally toward the end of the day going to pick up my dad from work and feeling so tired and all the city blocks seemed like a mile long, you know, being a kid. I remember getting grumpy, nothing seeming quite right. It was fun, it was exciting, but it was so overwhelming. Usually I started to cry. Well, come to think of it I guess that wasn't so happy either.

What else? Other happy times as a kid.—Melissa laughed.—I don't know. It doesn't seem like there are so many.—Oh, OK. Getting a puppy. That was kind of neat. There was this pet shop that my mom and I used to go to. Sometimes there'd be an animal there that you could almost feel you were going to take home, but not quite. But then one day there was this little German shepherd puppy that my parents saw. I guess they kind of wanted the dog for safety more than to have for a pet. But I remember the excitement of getting a new pet. I remember going down to look at it one day and playing around and feeling like you got a new friend. And the anticipation of wanting to go back next day and pick it up, or just see the little thing. And finally the next day came, and we brought the puppy home, and it was a really neat feeling. I'd wake up in my bed at night and know he was still down there, and he'd be there the next day and the next, and it was a really neat feeling. I didn't know there was going to be the flip side later, when the dog got too big, and they decided to give it away. That was really sad—She laughed.—For every really neat thing, there was some equally shitty thing, seems like.

Jimmy was smiling; he was leaning back against a column of washing machines, fingering Melissa's memories as though they were breasts, the softness and succulence of them; he could twist them into different shapes as he sucked on them; he kissed their round pink areolae of sadness and tried not to mind them; he squeezed them and their nipples budded.

Let's see, Melissa said. What else? Oh, OK. Going to the movies as a kid was a big thing for me, going on Saturdays and in the afternoon. It was different than when you went with your parents. Adults seemed much bigger than they were, from a kid's eyes. You'd tilt your head up to look at 'em and it was like looking at a redwood tree or something. In the afternoon there was nothing but kids, people your size, going to see all the same stupid movies. It was a neat feeling to sit there with your popcorn and whatever you bought. You had your own money, and you could buy whatever junk you wanted to buy. You didn't have to listen to your mom and dad tell you don't get that junk. You could just eat and eat and eat and eat whatever you wanted, until you got sick. That was neat. It was also a neat feeling being able to crawl around the movie theater in the dark, being able to go upstairs and spook yourself out on the balcony and play with your friends.

A neat thing I tripped on when I was young was the feeling you got from going into unique little places you'd never been before. Like I remember the first time I found a creek that was by my house. It was like my own private little place. I felt like I was the first person ever to find this place. I remember the smell of it. It just smelled so wet and damp and neat. If darkness could have a smell, it seems like being by the creek smelled dark. The trees and the sound of the water and the squishiness under your feet had a dark smell to it that was nice. But it also had a new feel to it like something exciting that had never happened before. I don't feel that so much as an adult. In fact I don't feel that much at all.

Let's see. What else? Uh, happy happy happy happy happy . . . Hmm. Gosh, this is getting hard now.

That's when it gets interesting, said Jimmy.

28

The whore laughed nervously. I don't know, she said. I had a really kind of uninteresting childhood. I wasn't from a big family. I was the only one, actually. The only child, so there wasn't a whole bunch of horsing around. It seems like looking back on childhood all the small things seem really small.

Goofing around in church, that was fun. Getting someone else to laugh, or having a little joke, or you knew and your friend knew when you gave him that signal that that was what you were supposed to think about. Little rush of good feeling you got from doing it and knowing that somehow it was kind of wrong, and somehow that made it all the more exciting.

Was tricking fun for you like that? said Jimmy. (He was an optimist too.)

Well, it's never really been *fun*, Melissa said. Most of the *fun* I get out of it's the money.

Later he said to himself after all they're her memories not Gloria's but then he said after all I paid for them.

What else? said Melissa sighing to herself when he left her. Happy happy stories.

Home again

Jimmy went back to the Hotel Bailey, where he was staying for eighty-five dollars a week, and Pearl looked up from the TV program she was watching and smiled at Jimmy with her snaggly old teeth because Pearl was always friendly and nice and Jimmy said hey Pearl any messages for me? and because Pearl was so nice she made a show of looking in Jimmy's mailbox and said no I thought maybe there was something but not today I guess, and Jimmy sighed and said I was hoping maybe Gloria might have gotten in touch with me and Pearl said not today and Jimmy said here's my rent for the next three days and Pearl said thanks honey I'll give it to the boss and Jimmy said well I guess I'll go up and use the bathroom and Pearl said so you want some toilet paper then? and Jimmy said yeah and Pearl tore off a nice long hunk for Jimmy and passed it to him through the window. — (At the Hotel Bailey they had given up keeping toilet paper in the bathroom because as fast as they put it there it got stolen.)

Jimmy went upstairs and used the bathroom and went down the hall along the sea of old carpet that looked like lichen and dog hair and came away under his shoes as he stepped on it. He met a man standing in the center of the corridor and Jimmy said excuse me and the man didn't say anything so Jimmy went politely around him and unlocked the door of 108 and went inside where his stinking bed waited to embrace him.

Gloria

Now he remembered being five when Gloria was three and they took a train ride to Louisiana to see Gloria's great-grandmother, who was dying, and Gloria was hopping around the car like a sparrow so that Gloria's mother kept saying just calm yourself girl but Gloria said I want to jump as high as the tops of the mountains! and Jimmy said you be a mountain and I'll be a cloud so Gloria put her hands over the top of her head in a point like a steeple and said, see I'm a mountain and Jimmy puffed out his cheeks and blew her hair around and said see, I'm blowing over you to give you snow and Gloria rushed to the window to see snow and it was snowing then just like Melissa said. Gloria's mother said child don't reach out the window you'll fall out, but when she wasn't looking Jimmy stuck his hand out and caught snowflakes to give Gloria and then Gloria laughed. — When they were a little bigger Gloria and Jimmy used to go through the woods to a little brook where nobody had ever been before and the sky was so blue when they found it again beyond the raspberry brambles and there were water-striders in the little pools and Gloria said look how they live in bubbles all the time, I wonder if the bubbles are soft and Jimmy found caddis-worms building houses for themselves out of colored pebbles and some days they went upstream, leaping along the smooth flat boulders in the creek that helped them like water-stairs, and they passed an old house that the trees were growing through and then at last they came to the dam, which Gloria said was the end of their territory; other days they went the other way until the river flattened and widened in slow bends full of suckered carp and great clay cliffs rose above the plain with pine trees along the backbone of the ridge so that Jimmy and Gloria felt like grand explorers; there they used to make faces and idols out of the wet clay and leave them in the sun to dry until next time when the idols were hard and hot and smooth-baked. Then Jimmy was a little afraid and he said Gloria are they alive? and Gloria said oh, Jimmy, don't you know what alive is? *I'm* alive! and she jumped so high in the air and her face was in the sun and Jimmy cried *I'm* alive too! and he jumped even higher, and then they found a big warm flat rock in the middle of the river and lay down on it eating the sandwiches their mothers had made for them.

5

Code Six

The next morning Jimmy was feeling troubled in his mind despite the happiness of the river, because there was something funny about fucking Melissa's memories instead of her cunt and then too he didn't know what to do with the memories that hadn't been made into Gloria's like the one about going to movies and sitting by herself in the darkness eating popcorn which couldn't really be Gloria's because he wasn't in it and anyhow *could* the memories ever be Gloria's and would she keep accepting them and what if the wrong one contaminated her like Melissa's German shepherd who kept barking and whimpering in Jimmy's nightmares (and he heard Melissa crying also when the dog got too big and her parents had to give him away and Melissa's mother said now stop that or I'll give you something to cry about and the dog kept running away from his new owners and coming back and scratching at the front door whining in the night and Jimmy woke up and was sure he heard the dog sobbing underneath the bed and he actually got up and turned on the light before he realized that it was just the whore downstairs with a customer and he sat blinking on his mattress and shaking his head and scratching at the insect bites on his legs and thinking: Christ I sure am glad I didn't give that dog to Gloria because even she wouldn't have been strong enough to keep it from being taken away howling and howling so sadly!) and Jimmy sat wondering what to do, James, what to do, so when it was midmorning and the alleys were hot and stinking he set out to see his old friend Code Six, who lived on Sixth Street.

The whole world was sleepy and crabby. The Vietnamese grocers rolled up their steel shutters with a slam and sat behind their cash registers, heads in hands, and an early bird whore stood on the corner yawning and scratching; for everyone who mattered these bright hours were but a wait until the shutters clicked up behind the eyelids of Spider the Pimp and his broad whore-wife they called the Hog, and Phyllis and Regina and Jimmy who grunted oof oof at the spot of beer-hurt at the back of his neck like an inner boil which could never be excised but he was very patient. Before he'd walked two blocks, the sunlight had begun to hurt his eyes and forehead so he stopped at a pay phone and called Gloria, not that he had anything new to say but it was easy like Melissa's brown tit slopping out of the striped blouse, Melissa turning her neck to tauten it, and then after he'd kissed the receiver goodbye, trying not to smell the breath of previous callers, he lingered as if he'd forgotten to do something when the truth was only that he was shy about his errand like a pom-pom girl who's never even had her cherry popped; *Jesus* James he said to himself you're putting on such a bad show anybody who paid is gonna want his money back! because he had gotten out of the habit of asking anyone save Gloria for advice but in this matter . . . —and of course it would hardly do to ask Gloria; that would be like asking her what surprise he should get her for Christmas, so he walked more and more slowly and took a roundabout way of sidewalks and alleys, nodding at everyone he saw. —No one nodded back.

Now let's calculate it fine, thought Jimmy to himself. What am I going to tell him exactly? Do I need to tell about how it first came to me in the clinic when I thought that maybe Nicole gave me some disease? No, that's not his business. I don't want that thing about disease getting around. I'd better not say anything about that.

But I do have to tell him what's happened since it came to me. About her. He knows her. It won't be bad.

33

I don't know why it *seems* so bad all of the sudden. It's not like he and I keep secrets from each other.

He plodded past the massage parlor on Larkin and turned the corner where a rusty Lincoln sat beside the street wall watching him through its shattered windshield. The car had been abandoned months ago and was not really good for much except fucking in which many people had done or else the gentle lycanthropy of transvestites who ducked in to adjust a new wig and pat makeup on under the guidance of the mirror on the sun visor in the passenger side; no one had smashed that yet. The black whores from Oakland also used it sometimes to change hair and dresses one two three times a night when they or their pimps robbed tricks. Jimmy had never paid much attention to the Lincoln until Code Six found a full bottle of Thunderbird in a paper bag, right beside the bumper. — Now it kind of gives me a feeling that Larkin Street is Larkin Street, said Code Six. — After that, Jimmy had a good feeling whenever he saw it. He laughed inside himself and kicked the sagging tires. — That was a good thing you did for my friend, he said.

He ambled past the junk shops, the gilded eagle shops, the shops that sold toys which would break right away, the ripoff hardware stores that sold flimsy locks for too much, the boarded up shops in whose doorways leaned ironing boards and broken bicycles, Jimmy thinking, Lord I am *rolling* along. It was very hot. On the sidewalk, a shitty kleenex did not stir. He saw Spider the Pimp and said top of the morning! but Spider just spat. He passed a sign that said HELP WANTED and said yeah, *right* but then he remembered and stroked the blue-grey stubble on his chin and said hmm. With both of us working, thought Jimmy excitedly, and her so quick at learning everything, we'll be able to buy that house so soon that Code Six's head'll spin and we'll give him the spare room if he promises to clean himself up and every day I'll come down to the Tenderloin and give money to my friends who right now are sleeping like invisible stars all around us.

Yeah *right*.

Gloria? What can I do to make you happy, Gloria? You're not crying anymore, are you? Gloria?

Well, I was feeling good for a minute there.

He crossed Market Street and passed the Vietnamese restaurant in front of which old Richard saluted him with a crutch saying hey Jimmy nice day ain't it? and Jimmy said can't complain and ducked between two piss-stained buildings where he knew his friend would be. Behind the dumpster, Code Six sat with crossed legs scratching and muttering inside the shelter of his overcoat, which was where he lived. He was big and fat and had yellow teeth and his body odor was so strong that at night you could practically find him in an alley by smell. He wore a jacket that might have been brown or green; if you brushed up against it brown stuff or green stuff smeared off on you.

Code Six had been a straight sucker until he got to Nam. He and Jimmy had served together in 1968, right before the Tet thing happened and the boys started coming home in flag-wrapped boxes. Once Code Six and Jimmy got their discharges they used to watch television together at Code Six's house on Florida Street because every time they turned on the television they saw the generals sauntering up out of the helicopter together with their hands in their pockets, while their aides walked respectfully behind and Code Six said Jesus remember when we saw *him*?, and the generals did not do anything as crude as smiling at the cameras or slapping each other's shoulders because they were already as comfortable with everything as old men in summer sitting on the front porch and Code Six said *man* that's some fuckin' *generals* there, James! and Jimmy said yeah I'm gonna open you up another beer; so, hands swinging, the generals strode up to their MEN, turning their heads briskly from side to side whenever they spoke so that they could look into every

35

soldier's eyes—and Code Six watched the screen with eyes shining and said let's stay busy *fightin'* to preserve this god-damn *land*, and keep this fuckin' *flag* up high! and Jimmy said oh *fuck* the flag;—*thank you!* said Code Six sarcastically; you say *fuck* the flag; I say stop *fuckin'* with me! and Jimmy said pass me another beer.

Code Six and Jimmy were not and never had been cadets immaculate in long white sweeps of uniform; they were the *troops* silhouetted black against the blue sea, the troops leaping down from the landing craft into the hot sea, running toward the beach, the soldiers running through a burned-out place where pale faces prayed over the dead bodies that kept coming back inside plastic bags inside caskets inside flags in a truck with everyone saluting; will you *look* at those new Hueys! shouted Code Six and of course there *were* helicopters spinning, making the grass whirl, and soldiers leaped out so quickly and the side-doors slid shut again and the helicopters rose and the grass rose again;—oh, *there* are some soldiers, thought Code Six as he watched, soldiers like Jimmy and I were, fighting the fucking GOOKS and SLANTS and SLOPES, soldiers trotting single file across a smoking field; and from the air the television showed fire blossoming tightly in NVA towns and in great puffy random mushrooms in the jungle as the soldiers slammed huge rounds into the big bucking gun and smoke rose like mist, but it was all silent; it was a rule of Code Six's in those days to keep the volume turned to zero because certain sounds from Nam gave him nightmares and certain things the generals said made him mad (but nowadays people are always getting outraged by something, as letters to the editor show) and Jimmy didn't care whether the world was loud or silent, so they sat on the couch in Code Six's place in perfect content-ment and Code Six's wife said I don't know *why* you two always watch that stuff I mean you've done your bit haven't you and Code Six said don't you tell me what to fucking watch you bitch what the *fuck* do you care so Code Six's wife

36

slammed the bedroom door and started crying so Jimmy said can we turn the volume up now pal and Code Six said no fucking way so Jimmy said pass me another beer and leaned back on the couch trying not to listen to Code Six's wife-sobbing behind the bedroom door and therefore watching with ever increasing attention the soldiers leaning back in the tall grass, firing their assault rifles soundlessly, then running back to the safety of the helicopter when it came, each soldier helping his comrade in. In a field, soldiers rose as slowly as bomb-smoke from their hiding places. The low squat helicopters ranged through the sky in swarms, with their tails up behind them, as if they were dragonflies. Long orange lines came shooting down, illuminating a village (and watching from the open bay of the plane, the television showed the puffs and trails of bullets). The long lean bombs went swimming slowly downward like fish, until they came to the towns and became orange flowers. In the jungle there were no marks except roads and craters. — The television also showed the big eggheaded politicians, who were as energetic as the generals but whose energy turned more toward friend-liness than theirs. They were always shaking hands (the family present, the wife's little hand taken protectively in two of the politician's great ones); they were always kissing little girls after being sworn in.

So Jimmy and Code Six went back a long way. Fucking A!

Code Six didn't have his television, his couch, his wife, or his house on Florida Street anymore. Jimmy came down with a fifth of Night Train for him because Code Six drank port now; it was a cheaper drunk than beer.

Now *there's* my fuckin' *soldier*! cried Code Six in delight, whapping Jimmy on the back as they stood between the trash cans where the police couldn't see and Jimmy took a pull on a Budweiser in a paper bag and Code Six opened his Night Train and gulped it, and Jimmy said now Code Six I want your input on something and Code Six said man don't bother me with input and that catshit like some beady-eyed chaplain because I see snakes and I see *dragons* and Jimmy said sober up and Code Six said I'm as sober as *you* ya stupid drunk and the only advice or *input* I have to give you is empty your bowels before combat check your M-16 for jams and kill all the fuckin' *slopes*!

Jimmy said listen bud I want your input about Gloria.

Oh, said Code Six mildly. That's different. We all know how you feel about that. He licked the rim of the bottle and set it gently down between two trash cans. That was good, he said. Thank you.

Listen, Jimmy said, I told you how I'm always dreaming about her so she won't leave off bothering my sleep and thinking how to be true to her and being aware of how happy she always is.

So get laid or jerk off, said Code Six. What do you need *advice* for?

Well, said Jimmy, I'm looking for her and I've got to find her and I'm using those whores to help me but is it *right*? I feel so confused in my mind about it. Do you hear what I'm saying? and Code Six said no and Jimmy said you hear what I'm saying and Code Six raged and said stop talking like a fuckin' *slant* with all your Chinaman's circumlutions say what you mean and mean what you say, so Jimmy took a deep breath and hanging his head a little bit explained exactly what he was doing and planned to do with the whores and Code Six laughed and said oh purple hearts of purple *Jesus* and Code Six said oh shit and Code Six said OK, some advice actually comes to mind right now. But you gotta keep it to yourself, Jimmy, because I can't get involved. I mean, I have a habit to support. Am I clear?—Yeah, Jimmy said.

Well, said Code Six, if the cops get wind you're obligated not to use my name, or nothin' like that.

I promise, said Jimmy.

See, *that's* a fuckin' *guy* here, man! cried Code Six admiringly. A good reporter, he don't give up his sources!

Don't *reveal* nothin', agreed Jimmy.

Code Six cackled: He'd sit in goddamn jail till . . . till that *old-ass* buildin' there fell down in the street!

And *crumbled*, Jimmy shouted, opening another beer.

And *fucked* everything up before he . . .

At the *very least*, Jimmy said.

OK, said Code Six. I tell you my advice.—Oh, shit, here comes those dragons again. I never would've believed I'd see dragons. Not that they're dragons really; that's just what I call 'em. Jimmy, you think you kin buy me another jug? No? OK. I tell you my advice anyway.

Shoot, said Jimmy.

You want my advice? said Code Six.

Jimmy said let's have it, fella.

Well, said Code Six, my advice is go ahead and *use* those bitches and take everything you need from 'em make their hair Gloria's hair if that's what you gotta do make their eyes Gloria's eyes an' feel free to cut their motherfucking *cunts* out!

6

The Coral Sea

At the Coral Sea bar on Turk Street the men were drunk and friendly and said where you from and Jimmy said from here and one guy said he was from New Mexico and Jimmy said say fella do you know where Cuba, New Mexico is? and the man said sure do and Jimmy said my ex-wife and I took a train ride through New Mexico once on the way to Louisiana and I remember we stopped there yes I think was Cuba and bought some Indian jewelry you know that turquoise and silver stuff—of course that was over twenty years ago now. — The guy said you don't look that old, but on the other hand I look older than I am so I guess that makes up for it.

On his way out a drunk said look at this! and Jimmy saw a military patch on the drunk's shoulder and the drunk cried *Eighty-Second Airborne!* and Jimmy laughed and punched the guy on the shoulder, right on the patch, and they both shook hands.

The Queen of the Tenderloin

On Jones Street Jimmy met a lovely black whore who stood smiling at him and fixing her hair and he could just imagine ripping her panties off and spreading the cheeks of her ass and giving it to her right up the butt and he said to her wow you are *so* beautiful you are the Queen of the Tenderloin and the whore said big deal that means I'm the Queen of

Nothing and Jimmy laughed and laughed and said yep you whores always have all the answers.

Gloria

Then Jimmy remembered his purpose and he went down to the Nitecap on Hyde and O'Farrell, seeing across the street Melissa waiting with slender legs drawn very close together and high heels shining as white as new ice on the sidewalk which was stained with giant figures like something pouncing on something, and Melissa had drawn her arms in and was looking back over her shoulder at him with her lips parted, her lower lip parted, her teeth as white as her high heels, and her eyes were like mirrors in which he could see his affection so needfully reflected as she stood waiting with that eternal backward look, the darkness at the bottom of the hill ahead of her. Jimmy nodded at her and said without saying it Gloria thanks you. And I love you. It was and always will be a beautiful train ride. And he went around the block and came back to the Nitecap and sighted on a black whore who wore big dark sunglasses and he knew that she would cross the street to meet him, that she would be sweet and serious with him and he wondered so does that make her desperate? does it? she'll probably say to me she can't pay her rent for tonight unless she gets just forty more dollars, but is that being desperate if it happens to her every night or is she used to it like I'm used to it? Anyhow he thought it's time to see that loveliest thing in the world, the VAGINAL RAIN-BOW, the glory of cunt, cunt, cunt ... and her name was Dinah and he picked her up, semi-hard, and she took him to her hotel on Mason Street and Dinah was so happy when Jimmy got out his money. Dinah's pimp Jack was there, and he took the forty and went out saying enjoy yourself my friend and live long and prosper and then Jimmy said to himself doing what I am about to do I do for Gloria out of love for Gloria out of belief in Gloria, and Dinah said are you praying and Jimmy said oh baby hurry up and spread your legs and let me get *in* you.

Dinah

When they were done Dinah said give me ten dollars more and Jimmy said give me a lock of your hair to treasure forever and Dinah said if you love me you'll give me a tip and Jimmy said if you love me you'll give me a lock of your hair and also your nose and mouth and Dinah lay in bed pouting and said she was hungry and Jack said too bad I spent the whole forty on dope and Dinah said please gimme five dollars so I can have breakfast I'm so cold and so hungry and Jack said aw come on you're not gonna make a girl go hungry are you and Dinah shivered and wrapped herself up in blankets and Jimmy said I'll give you ten dollars for a lock of your hair and Dinah said no that's voodoo and Jack said stop whining you chocolate covered yummy little black bitch I'm gonna cut your hair now do you want length or thickness? and Jimmy said length is the primary consideration and Jack said where's that stiletto you had and Jimmy said the blade's pretty dull and Jack said never mind I have a razor and he pulled a long skinny lock of Dinah's hair straight up from her scalp and Dinah reached up and felt it and said that's too much! and Jack said never mind I was fixing to cut your hair anyway you'll never notice it and Dinah said what do you want it for anyway and Jack said to Jimmy I could tell just by looking at you you're a muff diver, I'm telling you Dinah is real good to eat out her pussy just pops and pops like popcorn and there are some times of the month when you could just light a match from her forehead she is so beautiful and Dinah screamed when Jack started sawing

42

across the hair with his razor and Jack said oh shut up you spoiled bitch and Dinah said you watch it or I'll show him my bruises and Jack said cut the crap with a butter knife and Jack said there you are I don't have a rubber band for it but I'll put it away for you all nice in a matchbox.

Home again

Hey there Jimmy you look happy said Pearl and Jimmy said oh Pearl the best damn thing happened today better than a whore with two cunts I was walking down Sixth Street and ran into my old buddy Code Six that I was in the service with and he said he had met *Gloria* last week and she was thinking about me! (I guess she tried to get in touch with me when I was at the Hotel Canada but I didn't have my forwarding address) anyway she gave Code Six this lock of hair for me to remember her by.—Jimmy I'm *really* glad for you, smiled straggly-haired old Pearl. Hey, boys! Did you hear that Jimmy and Gloria are getting back together?—But although there were half a dozen men in the lobby no one answered because no one cared.

Dinah and Jack

The saddest thing was when Dinah smiled widely or laughed on the bed with her legs spread, as if she were having a good time in that room full of dirt and steam and the radiator hissing and clanking. Her bed was three canted mattresses; the dresser was missing a drawer, and there was a bloody tissue on top of it, and the walls were bare. Jack sat on the bed, shooting speedball into his arm, and Dinah yawned and scratched her itchy cunt.

Gloria

The young girl stood half in a rectangle of sunlight on a wall, hands on hips, holding a beer in a paper bag, and the knife of light slit her down the middle so that under the nightgown one breast was bright and one was dark and the knife sliced down the shorts she wore (the tail of the night-dress tucked in), and with two fingers she plucked one cuff away from the other to accentuate her crotch which the knife sliced through and down between her legs and she was very majestic and mysterious as she stood proudly half-faced in the light. And her pride was firstly that she could make almost any man's dick hard, and secondly that when men fucked her she lay perfectly still and her thoughts were somewhere else, so that the rasp of drunk-breath in her face was no closer to her than the patter of raindrops on the roof when she was sleeping. For we all must build our worlds around us, bravely or dreamily, as long as we can we shelter ourselves from the rain, walling ourselves in gorgeously.

Gloria

Although buying Dinah's hair had been an escalation of sorts, Jimmy had no intention of taking Code Six's advice literally, buying whores' dirty panties and kissing them (although when a whore talked he thought this is what Gloria would have said, and suddenly he was all attention; when a whore stripped he thought Gloria would have had underpants like this, and then he had to pay for them), of buying whores' dresses and high heels and garter belts, wigs and bras and socks and similar items each representing some woman's physical character like notes of music, which are no less pure, distinct, unique for not meaning anything (as long as the panties that were to become Gloria's smelled like some particular cunt it did not matter which because that was now Gloria's cunt; the only important thing after that was consistent obedience to precedent); certainly he never wanted to go farther like Jack the Ripper and hack off parts of whores' bodies to take home with him, as if through some combination of hubris and sincerity he could construct, however momentarily, his own charnel-Gloria like some Frankenstein's monster lying in his bed and listening for him with black girls' and white girls' ears in its patchwork face and grinning for him with Cecily's teeth and Dinah's teeth and Phyllis's teeth and licking its grey quilt of lips with Melissa's pickled tongue. No, if he'd done that people might have *asked* about her, although Jimmy was certainly ready to explain if anyone did ask which no one did that Gloria was going through some changes right now so she never did anything in fact she hardly ever talked and if Jimmy went to the bars

Gloria would stay home in bed or else she would wait across the street in one of the abandoned cars; whenever she saw Jimmy with other people she hid. But these apologetics would have been embarrassing. Besides, they were unnecessary. Whenever Jimmy needed the smell of a woman or the soft weight of a woman's embrace, why, he had the whores being themselves for Gloria who partook of them all and lived on them all like some sky-goddess feasting upon the smoke from sacrifices. As for the rest of what he needed, the airy loveliness and happiness, he had that always with him; it floated at his arm like a helium balloon; no one could see it or ask about it or take it from him. So, having the hair, he really only needed the memories. Jimmy sat alone in his room, drinking tequila until his lips went numb. That's right honey babe (he said to Gloria) I have you I'm not lying I never lied to you I haven't told the truth for so long now that I've given up lying.

The Black Rose

Jimmy and Code Six strolled into the Black Rose a week later, on a Saturday afternoon when things were just starting to perk up and some lovely transvestites were dancing on the stage beside the pay bathroom and all the girls made a face when Code Six walked by and they wrinkled their noses and fanned the air away from themselves in a most ladylike way and said Jesus girl he stinks and Code Six went to the bathroom and reached for a dime to unlock the door but saw that his pocket was empty so he stood waiting until a man came out and then said well *thanks*, pal; I guess I came at the right time, and the man didn't say anything but Code Six caught the door before it closed and went inside and took a long piss as he read the competing slogans on the condom dispensers.—Sure is a nice day, Code Six said to the urinals. I never thought James would take me around again. But he don't care no matter how bad I smell; a friend sticks by a friend.—Meanwhile Jimmy was at the bar passing the time by asking Cecily if she had seen Puerto Rican Phyllis whom he had first met that night before he flatbacked Nicole; but Cecily was cool to Jimmy for some reason and did not prove informative; when Code Six came out of the bathroom it became clear by the way Cecily held her nose that he was the reason so Jimmy quickly said open me up a Budweiser would ya Cess but Cecily said is *he* drinking too? and Jimmy looked down at the floor and said I don't know (knowing perfectly well that Code Six was not because Code Six did not waste his money in bars) and Cecily said if he's not drinking he can't stay, and Jimmy said well cancel the beer

I guess we'll just have to leave then; and he strode about the bar in the most earnest possible way until his eyes rewarded him with a view of Phyllis sitting in the corner, twirling and twirling the straw in her pink lady. Then suddenly he realized that he had not just been passing the time. When are you coming? he said inside himself. Will this one make you come sooner? You know ever since Nicole I never stopped thinking about you.

So you don't want me to drink with you? said Code Six.

No, it's not that, said Jimmy. But I have to find her.

You found her, looks like. Sure are staring at her.

You know who I mean.

Well what the hell did you drag me out of my turf for? I thought you said you wanted my company.

I didn't think it through, said Jimmy steadily.

Code Six smiled. Don't think about it, he said. It's what you need to do. Well, uh, full auto fire, huh?

I'll come find you later, said Jimmy. Here's a buck for wine and thanks for everything.

Keep your fucking buck, said Code Six. What do you think I am, a charity case? You're the charity case.

Phyllis

Phyllis said yeah, what do you want? and Jimmy said are you working? and Phyllis said oh and Phyllis said *oh* and Phyllis said oh, honey I could make you so happy and she put Jimmy's hand on her breast and made him knead it and Jimmy said nice stuff Phyllis, really nice and then they went outside.

In the windowpanes of bars all around the blue neon Budweiser signs, reflections made cool jungles in which blurs pursued blurs.

After Jimmy zipped his fly back up Phyllis got to her feet

49

and Jimmy said I have more money Phyllis if you come and meet a friend of mine, and Phyllis said how much and Jimmy said twenty and Phyllis said forty and Jimmy said thirty and Phyllis said anything for you.

Dinah and Phyllis

Dinah leaned up against the wall on one leg, smiling and wearing mirror sunglasses (sunglasses make the world quieter and safer, as if you are viewing things behind smoked windows fronting your skull-house: you are inside and the world is outside, and the world cannot see into you; mirror sunglasses double the armor), and she wore a man's crewneck shirt to show her chest off and her legs were bare and her hair glowed around her like a corona. Her tits were goose-pimpled with the cold. She wore shell earrings that swung with her hair like satellite moons. She stood and waited until she saw a police car coming; then she walked slowly away in the center of the broad broad sidewalk, wiggling her ass while an old man sat on two steps watching her and smoking a cigarette.

That's her, said Jimmy.

Phyllis said how much is she getting and Jimmy said forty and Phyllis said then give me forty and Jimmy said anything for you.

Hey Dinah said Jimmy I want you to meet my friend Phyllis, and Dinah and Phyllis looked at each other, and Dinah said to Jimmy well what's up babe oh now I remember you you're the one that cut my hair well it grew back so do you want another date?

I do said Jimmy and I remember *you* because you're so beautiful Dinah I'm telling you I'll never forget the first afternoon I saw you when you were at that fire hydrant in front of the Nitecap with your head so straight and proud

50

and you looked so fine and your thighs were so soft and not too thin not too fat and the street was reflected in your mirror sunglasses but curving away crazily.

The way you flatter me, laughed Dinah.

I mean it, said Jimmy, and Phyllis is just as beautiful as you, so let's all three go up to your place and *relax*.

How much? said Dinah.

Forty, said Jimmy.

And forty for me, reminded Phyllis as she slid her arm around his waist.

Yes, it was a sunny happy day, happy as a whore down on hands and knees to make you laugh in the doorway of a hotel, wiggling her shiny satin ass, and the laces of the whateveritwas dug into her flanks going back and forth like bootstrings, funny as the doggishly ugly faces of fortyish transvestite whores pursing their cheeks and loudly wolf-whistling at men whom they thought might just might want to have their dicks sucked, transvestite whores alone or in pairs or even in threes playfully slapping each other's paunches with fat arms, showing off their hormone tits with winks and calls and looks from side to side to make sure that Laredo and the other undercover bitches weren't rolling down the street in a van or an old junker that tried so hard not to look anything like the standard black-and-white that had busted and would bust every last one of them, over and over, confiscating their money when they caught them in the act.

Is this some three-way scene? said Dinah. You want me to fuck her or you want more hair or what?

I want you both to tell me stories, said Jimmy.

That sounds like a fun date, said Dinah. Even better than the last one. You are *so* creative. I *love* men with new ideas.

They went to the Hotel Cheyenne and because it was after visiting hours Jimmy had to give the clerk five dollars and then they went upstairs and Phyllis and Dinah said not a word to each other and Phyllis sat down in her tank top with

a single lock of hair curling over her forehead and gazed
sadly at the wall and Dinah smiled at him brightly, putting
all of herself into it because she had not yet been paid, and
Jimmy said all right now honeypies sit on that bed and take
your clothes off and Phyllis undressed and bounced her big
tits in her hands with her eyes on Jimmy so trustingly and
her penis was hard between her legs and Dinah pulled her
dress over her head and sat down watching Jimmy with her
fresh stare and her beautifully pouting lower lip. She lay back
on the bed and started playing with a roll of toilet paper.

Ladies you are BEAUTIFUL, Jimmy declared; ladies you are
PERFECT.

Honey you want me to play with myself while I tell you
stories? said Phyllis.

If you want to, girl, said Jimmy. That's your decision. Just
tell me stories about things that have happened to you.

Phyllis

When Phyllis was little her mother used to paint her sister's
nails and Phyllis would be a-cryin' until she painted Phyllis's,
too. When she turned twelve she just kept thinking about
having a boy make love to her. She did it with her cousin,
and it was wonderful even though she didn't know anything
about lubrication or anything and she thought I know how I
am now and how I will always be. In high school with its
callowness and strictures she was just a regular gay boy
although she could already swoop her muscular arms in
gestures of spectral perfection that attracted respectful whis-
pers as did the special things Phyllis said and the special way
Phyllis walked so she was vulnerable because there was a lot
of jealousy among the queens, who would push you down
the stairs if they could or hurt you in some other secret way;
therefore Phyllis became secret, too, hid herself in herself

until 1969 when she was sixteen and the sun came up and spread its light in all directions like a bright yellow dress because Phyllis had met Shawna, who was a real transvestite, and Shawna saw the beautiful secret in Phyllis and looked into Phyllis's eyes knowing that she could let it out so that it could shout and dance and make Phyllis happy as Shawna was happy, Phyllis had never realized before that you could be that perfect. Shawna showed her everything, showed her how to dress and how to do it, and Phyllis started taking estrogen and Premarin® and Provera®* so that she got the sweet big breasts that men loved to squeeze through her shirt and one night she was ready to come out and so she and Shawna went out with some army men and told them watch this and they went into another room and changed and came back and the army men were drinking champagne and talking about jungles and helicopters, men and helicopters, smoke and flames shooting out of tanks and black smoke rolling over the jungle hills and stinking steam rising and animals crying and when Phyllis and Shawna swept proudly into the room the champagne glasses just fell from the army men's hands and they said is that *you?* and Phyllis was so proud and happy.

Dinah

The first thing Dinah could remember was riding in the back seat of the car with her sister when her mother drove down to Tijuana to go to the dentist and on the way back Dinah's mother gave them both gum because they'd been good and Dinah and her sister chewed their gum and had such a good time until their fillings popped out.

---

* i.e.: female hormone supplements. Premarin® is a brand name for estrogen: Provera® is a brand name for progesterone.

Phyllis

Phyllis's mother kept saying it's your life; it's your life; just don't mess yourself up. The first time Phyllis went out tricking she wasn't nervous because she thought she was just going along with Shawna to watch and learn. But somehow she ended up being the one to give the driver a blow job. He must have been able to tell that she was inexperienced, because when it was all over he said give me my ten dollars back and started shaking her and hurting her until she went to boohooing and gave him the money back and then he pulled over and let her out.

Dinah

I had this one Kung Fu master that loved to be my slave, laughed Dinah, yawning and stretching her body like a snake, scratching herself, lying naked on the bed with Jimmy's stiletto between her legs. — And he liked for me to tie him up and choke him around the neck, then make him suck my *toes* and things. And he wrote me out a contract for his life. — Dinah giggled. — And he said I could do whatever I wanted to do to him. I could rent 'im out to my friends an' I could beat 'im, and if he happened to die — *huh!* — he had my permission. I mean, I had his permission. I had this other date; he looked just like Kenny Rogers. And he would like for me to give 'im golden showers. He liked for me to drink like a sixpack of beer and then after about a good hour then he'd want me to piss all in his mouth and he'd gobble it down just as fast as I could piss it out.

Phyllis

Phyllis consulted Shawna and learned to use her lips less and her tongue more when she gave blowjobs so that her ratings steadily climbed right along with the drivers' penises, and her breasts were lovely but she kept *her* penis because as she said to Jimmy with a wink she got more attention with a penis. For a year or two she was working in a government office by day and whoring by night, and she was always yawning all day and making mistakes and rushing off excitedly to make money when evening came and *she* could come alive with lipstick waving to her pal Luna who lay on her side on the hood of Code Six's Lincoln spreading her white-stockinged legs in a scissors kick so that you could look right up her stained skirt and see the outline of her balls, and the other cars around her were like dirty white islands in the darkness, and Phyllis called Luna babe go ahead and bite their nuts off! and Luna laughed and called back I'm gonna pick their pockets too and buy me a heap of meth and groceries! and Phyllis clip-clopped perkily with racing heart to her own corner making music with the sexy click of her high heels and reaching out to cars until a car stopped and she got in saying honey I'm gonna make you *so* happy (but she always kept one hand on the doorhandle) and then the next day she'd come in to work so sleepy that finally the government said Phyllis dear you have two choices: quit or get fired; so Phyllis pouted and quit and started working out of her hotel room which cost sixty bucks a day but that was no problem because she shared it with three other Transformers who were as smooth and pure as chocolate statues, and in the morning Linda got herself takeout and Fawn and Luna took showers and made themselves up and rolled their deodorant on, and the hotel room was hot and sunny and clean and flowers yawned in the wallpaper and stuck out long delicate tongues of leaves and Linda smiled in her teddy bear

T-shirt and Luna watched television very quietly and Phyllis shot up and sat looking out at Eddy Street, at the Vietnamese children running, at the drunks shouting and falling while the sun poured itself into the hot pavement so that everything started to stink. At night Phyllis had some really good times.—Oh, she had such soft smooth arms! She looked really good now; a lot of the men she sucked off never knew she wasn't a woman. Some of them told her she gave the best blow jobs they'd ever had. One time when she went to jail someone who knew said she was a Transformer and they all said no fucking *way*; she ain't no Transformer; and when she was proven guilty of possession of a penis they said *wow*; they said that one ain't no Transformer—that one's a *Decepticon*!

Jimmy

The entire time he had been sitting on Jack's bed staring at the two women with round round eyes going *G-G-G*—and his grey hair jerking crazy as he rubbed his chin-sandpaper with one unconscious hand, breathing fast and hard as he concentrated so that Dinah thought to herself God look at that disgusting old pervert I wonder where he gets his money from and Phyllis thought well now I've seen both ends of him I have to say his face is even uglier than his dick! and Dinah thought Christ is he getting off just like that I wonder if he's coming in his pants I wonder if he changes his underwear afterwards God this is so stupid and Phyllis thought how much more money does he have? and Jimmy thought Gloria I can feel you kicking inside me like I was a woman and you were my baby Gloria I can feel you growing inside me please Gloria. And he thought I have Dinah's hair should I get something of Phyllis's? and he thought Phyllis go on and Dinah go on; tell me so I can keep going on.

Dinah

Oh, said Dinah, . . . and I had this one guy, a real nice healthy fine young guy, an' what he would like, he liked for me to kick 'im in his balls as hard as I can with my boots on. And then what he'd do is he'd ejaculate while I'm kickin' 'im. With my pointed-toe boots! You think you'd like that? You kind of remind me of that guy. I had another date, like with six-inch heels he liked for me and this other girl to walk all over 'is face with heels, and step on 'im as hard as we can, just walk like we're walkin' on concrete, an' step on his balls an' stuff with the heels. It didn't hurt—he came! An' lemme think. Let's see some other dates I've had.—Oh!—I've had dates they wanted me to screw 'em with dildoes an' vibrators, an' they wanted to suck 'em like they were suckin' on a man's penis. They wanted me to screw 'em with a dildo an' a vibrator, and whup 'em. I've had plenty of slaves. Then I've had plenty that wanted to give me pedicures an' kiss my ass and all kinda shit like that. But *that's* OK, 'cause they never been harmful.

Phyllis

Once Phyllis had a date who didn't know that she was a deceiver and she really liked him and he liked her and kept buying her drinks and feeling her and she pushed his hands out of her lap and she went with him and he really wanted it and she said she'd blow him but he wanted to stick it in real bad and Phyllis said not on the first date and he got mad and said what are you? are you a woman or not? and Phyllis got insulted and slapped his face and said don't you *talk* to a lady that way and how *dare* you and the man said he was sorry and Phyllis said take me home and the man said he was really sorry and Phyllis said take me home. He took her

57

home. The next week he called and Phyllis said what do you have to say to me and he said I'm terribly sorry and Phyllis said well I forgive you but I don't want to see you again and he said I'm horribly miserably sorry and Phyllis said all right come and pick me up. So he bought her drinks and cuddled up to her and Phyllis let him go a little farther and she could see he really wanted it so she said all right honey but I've got a surprise for you and he said what do you mean and she said I'm not what you think I am and when she showed him he was *flabbergasted*. But Phyllis said don't be afraid and she helped him and he went ahead and did it and thought it was wonderful. He fell hard for her. He was a married man with two kids, and he wanted to leave the family and come live with Phyllis forever. She finally had to break it off.—Oh, she was **GOOD!** (But Phyllis had needle tracks all over her arms.)

Dinah

Mmm, yawned Dinah. I had husband an' wives. Those benefit mostly for the wife. But I'm not into it. I'm not bisexual, or into oral sex as far as givin' it to another female. Once we been in a situation, then the husband wants to say it's for the wife and the wife wants to say it's for the husband. So then I end up with two or three hundred dollars—I have to think of stories now. I have to think of 'em.—OK, now, there been times when girls have gotten killed; the Vice have come by with pictures and stuff and showed 'em to us, like the Green River Killer when we were up in Seattle. There been times when I've cut . . . I've had to cut guys. Lot of 'em were, that's when I were drinkin'; that when I would get upset. Get vi'lent. 'Cause they'd get vi'lent with me. There was actually a time when I begged, actually *begged* this one guy not to get vi'lent with me, 'cause I *knew* what I would do.

It's happened plenty of times, believe me. This one guy, when I begged him, actually begged him not to get vi'lent with me, and I pleaded and I started crying because I was in such a depressed state of mind that I didn't care. So he wanted to get vi'lent with me, so I just started stabbing him. He went to the hospital; we both went in an ambulance, 'cause he pushed me through a two-storey window. I didn't go out the bottom floor; I just went out the large window, and I took off running and he came running up and he fell, and I waited for the police, and they found me, and they held me in jail twenty-one days to see if he died. Then they let me go, 'cause there were no charges or anything. It was self-defense.

Phyllis

Once when Phyllis was in a hotel she had a man up and he was crazy; he kept saying what do you *see*? and Phyllis said I see a bed and a lamp and a dresser and then he jumped on her and she screamed until the manager came. Once a man picked her up and got into the freeway lane and Phyllis said where are you taking me? and the man just stared at her as if he had never seen her before and she knew he was crazy and started boo-hooing and begging him to take her back or let her out but he just kept going right across the Bay Bridge and onto the freeway, faster and faster toward the Orinda hills where a whole mess of girls had just been found with their cunts cut out and the needle was steady at sixty and Phyllis started screaming oh my God and the needle was steady at sixty and the man stared and stared at her and they came to Orinda among the poppies and the buttercups and snapdragons that sparkled like night-cities in the hills above the freeway (at night the houselights came on like pale white moonflowers) and it was evening, the traffic all dun-colored on the grey concrete, winding up and up among the hills, the headlights like dim round cheeses, but the sun still caught the ridgetops, making the trees as rich an emerald green as blood was red, and the man took Phyllis higher and higher but she would never reach Mount Diablo where my friend Seth picked a bouquet of wildflowers for Maureen; and into Phyllis's head came a crazy voice saying of her, *Oh, she's headless—travelled a thousand miles without a head!* and Phyllis screamed please, oh my God and the yards were steep and ivy-glossy, and there were hedges on either side of the little streets, and it was very warm and the evening sun was orange and somewhere not far away there were pink lawn-geraniums and children playing basketball and the trunks of eucalyptus trees shimmered like skeletons and tall narrow white houses with orange roofs rose upon the hills and the man stared at her with inhuman eyes and the freeway was a dead permanent color and the tail-lights of the cars ahead of her were shining very red and bright like her screams that no one in the other cars could hear, and the sky was hot and bluish-white above her head but orange behind and purple before, and the lights of the cars began to glow brighter and brighter and Phyllis screamed and opened the door and jumped out and her wig flew off and she saw it flying as she flew and it looked very small on the shoulder of the freeway and then she hit and her adrenalin was going so fast she got right to her feet and she hadn't broken any bones but her face was laid open from *here* to *here* and she had a concussion and she saw the car speeding, speeding, away, with the passenger door flapping like a single tremulous wing.

Dinah

Once I went to jail and I got gang-banged, said Dinah brightly. Then she laughed. No, I'm lying. I'm lying.

Virtue is its own reward

Thanks girls, said Jimmy. Here's a ten dollar tip for *you* and for *you*.

Home again

Well Jimmy said Pearl you look all tired out. It's pretty late, too. What you been doing with yourself?

Oh I was out looking for Gloria again, he said, I met two friends of hers that had some information, so maybe if I think it all through I'll get a break. Was there any mail for me?

Let me see, said Pearl. There was something. Oh yes here's your disability check.

Jimmy went upstairs and locked the door. He took Gloria's hair out of the matchbox and kissed it. He lay down on the bed with his eyes closed.

Gloria

Jimmy did not want to think about the Green River Killer who had scared Dinah because that would scare Gloria, too, who was so innocent that on the train ride she kept saying I

see a green river out there I see a green *ocean*! when what
she saw was the greenness of Louisiana that rolled from
horizon to horizon with nothing in sight but a mangy dog,
Melissa's dog, that kept limping beside the train and howling
as if it knew someone and Gloria said why is he sad? and
Jimmy said he's just playing a game he's just chasing us for
fun and as soon as we get there he'll be there too and his
master will be waiting for him with a *big* bowl of dogfood;
and then they got to Gloria's grandmother's house and in
the guestroom Gloria said what do you *see*? and Jimmy said
I see a bed and a lamp and a dresser and Gloria said now
turn out the lamp and we'll sit here and pretend we're
watching movies all by ourselves now what movie are you
watching? and Jimmy closed his eyes and saw a man trying
to strangle Dinah and Dinah sobbing and struggling and
pulling her knife out and stabbing the man deep in the chest
so that his blood sprayed into her eyes and he came at her
clutching at her to kill her laughing and bleeding and saying
I am the Green River Killer and Dinah stabbed him again
and again and he pushed her through the window and Gloria
said why aren't you saying anything Jimmy why do you look
so strange what movie do you see? and Jimmy said I see a
movie about someone who likes people to walk on his face
but that's because he's made out of grass and he likes how
happy their toes are when they go barefoot and he likes it
when the rain falls on his face so he can grow taller and
greener, and Gloria said that's a good movie and Jimmy said
what do you see? and Gloria said I don't know it's all stories
and oh look here's grandmother's kaleidoscope now see how
the pretty things keep getting changed into something else.

Gloria

So when Jimmy was little he used to watch Gloria's mother painting Gloria's nails holding Gloria's hand over the bureau and buffing her nails with the sandpaper stick and saying Gloria, Gloria you've been biting your nails again and Jimmy said no ma'am it's from holding onto all those rocks at the creek and Gloria's mother said well whatever and she took the bright red nail polish that looked like candy (although the polish remover smelled better) and began painting Gloria's nails again so carefully and Gloria said I can see my face in my fingernails so little and reddish-pink and Jimmy would say paint my nails too and Gloria said yeah Mommy paint Jimmy too! and Jimmy would cry and cry until Gloria's mother painted his nails too but she would call him silly and say Jimmy you're a boy not a girl and so after a while Jimmy didn't ask to have his nails painted anymore. In the summer Gloria and her friend Shawna used to play in the rubber wading pool in the backyard and they would stay in there for hours pretending to be mermaids and calling each other mermaid names like Pearl and Crystal and Jimmy was jealous but Gloria said no you can't be a mermaid and Jimmy said aw why not and Shawna said he can get in too I don't care but Gloria said no he can't because you have to be a girl to be a mermaid and anyhow we don't have a third mermaid name to call him, so Jimmy had to run through the sprinkler and watch the rainbows in the arches of water that curved up into the air like silver ribs and they sprayed down on the newly cut grass that was so wet and made the bottoms of his feet green and Gloria laughed and said look at Jimmy running and Shawna said Jimmy can run so fast can't he Pearl and Gloria said yes so fast Crystal and Jimmy was still a little cross but later Gloria said I *want* you to be a boy not a girl and anyway I like you best of all.—Jimmy knew that that was true because she spent even more time with him than with

63

Shawna and would never take Shawna or anyone else to her and Jimmy's secret place that was down the steep path through the trees behind his house that led down through the raspberries and to the creek where they once saw an otter and another time a skinny black dog skulking along the ridge and following them all the way to the cliffs of clay so that Gloria was scared and said do you think it's a wolf do you think it eats people? and Jimmy said naw it's just a German shepherd without a home and Gloria held his hand and they made more clay people until Gloria turned sixteen and started spending more time with Shawna because Jimmy she said Shawna and I have girl-secrets and Jimmy was jealous of the two mermaids again but he didn't say anything and he watched how Shawna started teaching Gloria how to dress and how to walk and how to hold herself and how to keep her hand on the doorhandle when she got into a car with a stranger and overnight Gloria became even more beautiful as he had to admit and all the boys kept calling her but she said I only go out with Jimmy and the boys said Jimmy you prince are you porking her? and Jimmy said you bet I am every night but actually they'd never done it yet. One night Gloria got back late from band practice and she and Jimmy were supposed to go out to the movies and Gloria said gosh Jimmy I'm so sorry to keep you waiting give me fifteen minutes I'll be right back I PROMISE and Jimmy sat on the porch drinking a soda and watching the stars and humming *gol*-den times, *gol*-den times and nodding at the ghosts that leaned against houses and picket fences waiting with him as Gloria ducked under the fence into Shawna's back yard with new clothes under her arm, the price tags still on, and Jimmy saw the light go on in Shawna's bedroom and Jimmy said to the ghosts bet you want to date her too don't you, you assholes? until in fifteen minutes exactly Shawna and Gloria came over together laughing and Jimmy could not believe how beautiful Shawna had made Gloria so fast with a bow in her hair and a polka-dot dress and little red slippers and her eyes were snapping with pride and the two girls looked at the way Jimmy looked at Gloria and Shawna laughed and Gloria blushed and Shawna said well goodbye and Gloria hugged her and Shawna went home. That night he said Gloria Gloria you can do anything you want to me you can write a contract for my life or whatever because you know I'd die for you Gloria you're so perfect I'd even drink your piss and Gloria said Jimmy you don't have to talk that way aren't I going out with you? can't you see that I feel the same about you?

Later that night they had their first fight when Jimmy walked Gloria home and when he was almost at her house he started kissing her and kissing her and then he said Gloria I want to make love to you so bad and Gloria said I'm not ready I can't come to you yet until I remember everything and Jimmy said please Gloria do you love me or don't you? aren't I buying memories for you? then Gloria slapped his face and said how can you talk to me that way when you know that I do love you Jimmy and Jimmy said I'm sorry and Gloria said let me go this instant and don't say another word to me and she went inside slamming the door and Jimmy knew that she was crying. The next day he was forgetful at work and the boss said are you sick and Jimmy said sort of and the next day the boss said Jimmy pull yourself together and the next day the boss said Jimmy, I'll give you two choices: quit or get fired and the next day Jimmy knocked on the door and Gloria half-opened it and said well Jimmy what do you have to say to me and Jimmy said I'm sorry Gloria and she said I'm sorry I overreacted and she said come in and we'll talk about it and she said kiss me and she said come in here and close the door and now really kiss me.

11

Phyllis and Luna

Have you ever looked at an old street-whore's hand? Dirty worn creases deep as cuts, fingertips callused and peeling, thumb blackish-grey, but the whole hand so pale under the dirt, and so lean and tired like the wrist up which march buttons of sores . . . That hand has worked hard at giving love to strangers, or giving what strangers call love, or what strangers want instead of love—no, it *is* love because work is love no matter what or how.

Phyllis's hands looked like that.

Phyllis went home to Luna where they lay together with eyes glowing so lovingly because Luna had become a habit like the fire hydrant in front of the Nitecap that a million dogs had peed on, like the bus stop pole that Dinah had leaned against so long that she had worn away a palm-sized place in the yellow paint. Then Phyllis injected the smack very slowly into her vein, holding her breath to better appreciate the goodness and blessedness of it like Virgin Mary candy full of sunlight and ocean fruit, and she was happy until it wore off at which point she picked a fight with inoffensive Luna and then sat on the bed staring down at the night of parked cars and heavy barred gates of hotel lobbies and barred storefronts like jails and sidewalks empty where there was no business, corners packed with black men selling drugs, corners occupied by blondes wearily waggling ass, and Phyllis said they might as well just *lay* me in the *earth*! Of course there isn't even any dirt in this place, except on people's hands. Maybe they could bury me in shit. Plenty of that around here, at least.

Oh, stop your whining said Luna, who was still sulking.

You suppose there's anything after death? said Phyllis.

How the hell should I know? Why don't you just quit it. Whatever it is that you need to keep you going, figure it out and get it. It ain't me, girl, and it sure ain't your fix.

It's death, laughed Phyllis.

Oh, dry up, yawned Luna. Here, have a beer. Who were you with this afternoon?

That nigger bitch and a pervert that wanted his dick sucked. Later on he made us *tell* him shit. You know. Whatever it takes.

Luna went to the window.—You know that girl Nicole? she said. Well, she got stabbed.

Dead?

You hard of hearing or you just got cunts for ears?

Good riddance, said Phyllis after a while. She had AIDS anyway. I hate people with AIDS.

12

Jack and Dinah

Those Tenderloin hotel rooms were *havens*, not just worlds into which the Vice Squad looked and listened, bugging the elevators of the Hotel Canada for instance as everybody was convinced, so that Dinah was well aware that someday, some night, she might look through her window and see across the alley into a wall of many windows, and behind one of those windows the curtains would be drawn a little back and there she would see two glowing green circles like cat's eyes; but they were in fact Laredo's detective night-eyes, serenely horrible in their electronic night-vision goggles that magnified her in their circles as Laredo spread the curtains apart with her hands, not smiling, not frowning, but faintly green-glowing from cheek to chin like rotten algae ... yes, *this* hotel room was a real home — although, it is true, it was not a home of luxury where people could go to lie down when they were sick and listen to the soothing hiss of the tea-kettle, to watch their can of soup boiling on the stove when they were hungry and cold; but it was a home none the less; it was what Dinah and Jack had. If Laredo had in fact been surveying through her binoculars the ugliness of the room in the hotel where Dinah and Jack lived, with nothing in it, hardly, but a bed and a dresser and bloody scraps of toilet paper, she might have thought what animals, and how horrible, and what else is new, and when do I go back to Hawaii, until Jack got up and reached behind the window and brought over a record. No record player was anywhere near. The record was a version of Chopin's Nocturnes. It was Jack's favorite thing in the world. He read the performance notes on the jacket (which he knew almost by heart) and slid the record out a little so that its glistening blackness caught the light and then he pushed it back with his thumb and set the album behind the window again.

Dinah lay naked on the bed. Her body smelled like Jimmy's sweat. Her cunt was full of Jimmy's come.

I get hard just *looking* at you, Jack said.

Are you, dear? laughed Dinah.

We might as well play hide the salami, said Jack.

Dinah laughed. She clicked her stiletto in and out. Jimmy had given it to her. — Yeah, I like this, she said. Know what? I'd get a motherfucker and say come on motherfucker get with it gimme all your money gimme all your goddamned money right now. — She laughed and laughed.

Would you *stop* that? yelled Jack. Stop laughing like some goddamned *sheep*!

Dinah laughed and popped her stiletto in and out.

You sure are nothing to fuck around with, said Jack, half-amused. You're getting high fuckin' with that knife. Your little thing is starting to juice up and shit. Why, you vixen!

Jack

Jack looked great, although he had scars. He didn't have junky ways. He just had a 3 cc syringe. Every morning he woke up to something like morning sickness and had to get his speedball right away, but *he* wasn't addicted. If he didn't shoot up, on the first day his body would say all *right* you motherfucker I'm gonna GET you, but on the second day he would be OVER it, man; he would be healthy as pie.

69

Dinah

Leroy and Laredo caught Dinah the next night. — That's how it goes, said Leroy. Just remember the game. Tonight you got caught.

So what? Dinah said.

Tomorrow night you'll probably get away with it, Leroy said.

I'm not worried about it, Dinah said.

They drove her down to the station now, where streetlights shone down upon the sidewalk, and all the police cars were very black and white and logical.

You know what I want? Dinah said. I want to go to school at the community college with girls who think the worst thing in life is when their mothers won't buy them a new blouse. — Because she was drunk, she cried easily. — There are worse things in life, she said, but I don't want to think about 'em anymore.

Laredo and Leroy didn't say anything. They had heard that before.

Phyllis and her friends

Phyllis got busted, too—for smack. No one knew who'd snitched on her. Linda, Luna and Fawn moved out of the Hotel Canada. Linda and Fawn got busted or left town; no one saw them anymore. Luna moved to the Paradise Hotel.

The Kum Bak Club

Jimmy parked himself on a bar stool at the edge of a row of old men with round heads and glasses; their complexions were like tanned blankets. A few months back Jimmy had had a Korean whore who was real good and tight and he always used to tease her come on babe let's pop into the Kum Bak Club because that's Korean for come back isn't it and I'll always come back to you. — You *crazy*, laughed the whore, you just a big white *crazy* boy! — Ever since then Jimmy liked to drop by the Kum Bak Club once in a while. The whore always used to drink coffee there; she said their coffee was the best in the Tenderloin. During happy hour a Budweiser and a coffee were only two dollars. Jimmy ordered a Budweiser and a coffee and sat there drinking the Budweiser and the German barmaid asked him you vant a Glas? and Jimmy said thanks no and watched the steam rising slowly from the coffee that the Korean whore was never going to drink.

The Black Rose

Blinking lights rippled like domino stacks or windblown grass or a secret cipher of winking jewels, hard and round and yellow, with the wave of blinking sweeping across the top of the wide rectangular mirrors behind the bar and down their sides and under them and then the blinking lopped down between them like a descending ferris wheel at some night circus, curving below the glowing pinkish-purple square with the black rose on it, and the longer Jimmy stared at the black rose the more beautifully it glowed until it outshone the reddish warmth of the popcorn machine and the bloody-red light-globes on the ceiling that each hummed with its own little fan, and Jimmy had a Budweiser and tipped the pretty barman a dollar and sipped and sipped slowly and the sweet-malt taste of it with its chemicals and bad water was as natural in his mouth as the taste of his own breath and Jimmy watched the whores in the mirror; oh, there were so many interesting people there, hairstyles like cotton candy, and the video songs were loud and he felt the presence of people all around him being happy so that he was happy and he had another beer and a black girl who was really stacked set her money-tray down beside him and the lights flashed and everything flashed blue and red. But Jimmy wondered where Cecily was. He did not ask anybody. It did not matter that much. But he was used to her; he liked her.

Pretty little fishes

Jimmy walked up the hill on Jones Street to Ellis and on the way he saw a big pimp hitting a whore in the face saying oh you thought you could walk from me hah bitch? hah bitch? hah bitch? now you go out there and get some *money*! and Jimmy walked up Jones to O'Farrell and he saw a pimp being reasonable and explaining to his bitch no don't try it that way don't try to tell *me* how to cook pork feet and Jimmy walked up Jones to Geary and saw the most beautiful blonde he had seen all night with big strong thighs and a black miniskirt and he said how's it going but the blonde ignored him and Jimmy walked up Jones to Post and saw a grocery store on the corner and all the sudden a hankering came over him for a beef stick so he went in and a whore came in to buy cigarettes and when she came up to the counter, her pimp pushed his way through the men in line and took the pack out of her hands and opened it and pulled half a dozen cigarettes out and the whore paid with a twenty and the clerk was about to hand her a bunch of dollar bills with coins on top when the whore said you can keep the small change I can't carry it around with me, so the clerk dropped the coins back in the register and gave her the dollar bills and the whore lifted her leg as gracefully as a ballet dancer and let her shoe dangle on the ball of her foot and slid the money in.

Sebastian's

Jimmy walked up Jones to Sutter and stood looking into Sebastian's with its red-light globe like a flower, its watermelon-green one like a glowing bud, its green sphere and orange sphere, and men in business suits were leaning against the bar arguing, and Jimmy thought actually I feel kind of down I think I could use a drink, so he went into Sebastian's and sat down and noticed that all the men were looking at him and after a while the man next to him got up and moved his drink to another stool and Jimmy had a sick feeling wondering if they saw him as he saw Code Six who sometimes stood in the middle of sidewalk, grey-grimed with grief, wobbling on his legs, bending and muttering and stinking, and Jimmy sniffed at himself but he didn't smell bad, but some of the men laughed to see him sniffing himself, so he got up and left. The bartender had never served him.

The Coral Sea

Hey pal they all said to Jimmy when he swept triumphantly into the Coral Sea, and Jimmy took a seat at the bar beside a girl who sat bitterly stirring her drink and Jimmy thought at first that she was a whore and started talking to her but the girl just kept saying I'm *so* sick of myself and Jimmy said why sweetie what's so bad and the girl said no matter what I do I'm always lonely and I get attracted to men who don't care about me so they aren't there when I call them on the phone and Jimmy said now listen I used to be a sad sack myself until I met my wife Gloria who made me so happy she's always patient takes care of me when I'm sick buys me new clothes listens to me really listens not that she doesn't have her faults *everyone* has faults everyone's gotta stink sometime I'm not ashamed to admit it but Gloria's shown me how to squeak by and the girl looked him up and down saying what does she have that I don't? and Jimmy said probably *nothing* since as I can see you shoot from the *hip* (nice hip, too) and you *are* hip yep a straight-up gal a classy number number one and if I'd met you first I bet you could have made me just as happy well speaking of happiness can I buy you a drink? and the girl said please and Jimmy said another for her and three Budweisers for me. And just trying to enhance her evening he cried good for you sweetheart for saying please because please is the MAGIC WORD! She said why do I hate myself so much? and he pretended not to hear and gulped both beers down and felt a dry achey puckering behind his forehead, as if the beer were sucking things out of his brain.

I hate myself hate myself *hate* myself! the girl shouted, but everybody in the bar including Jimmy again pretended not to hear because it might be that her self-hatred was the base of her integrity which everyone had to have like that blonde whore Jimmy remembered from the time before Nicole, the

blonde whore who'd pulled her wedding dress down hunch-
ing her pale shoulders looking at him out of the corner of
her eye biting her lip and he saw the welts and scars of
beatings beatings beatings on her back and those were what
embarrassed her; that was how she kept herself, by being
embarrassed about being beaten when she was undressing
in front of strange men who were going to fuck her; once
Jimmy had seen and said nothing, she smiled at him so
gratefully and finished taking off her clothes, now relaxed
and basking in her sexual power over him just like all the
others . . .

Yessir, said Jimmy, I'll tell you, said Jimmy (gulping his
third Budweiser very thirstily), Gloria and I have known
each other since we were little kids. Can you *believe* that,
twinklepie? Some people think that kind of romance only
happens in stories but that's because they never get to know
their neighbors really know them in out in out which breaks
my heart because then they miss out on the best of life that
girl next door stuff know what I'm saying?

The trouble is, said the girl, in my hotel the room next
door is vacant. Somebody died in it. They sealed it up. Aside
from that your idea's bloody brilliant.

How about the *other* side of you? said helpful Jimmy.
Maybe he hypothesized there's some guy in there looking at
you through a hotel in the wall every night thinking wow
what a peculiarly pretty little pussycat if only I could screw
her inscrutable I'd have it made, and if you go with him first
thing you know sugardoll down comes the happiness curtain.

Mister there is no other side of me. I live at the end of
the hall.

Well said Jimmy there's always the fire escape just kidding
see what happened was our mothers were friends. That made
it easier I guess. So we were always playing together come
to think of it I can't remember when Gloria wasn't with me.

I thought little boys and little girls were supposed to hate
each other, she said. *I* hated boys.

Maybe that's your problem hon because what this world needs is *more* love three times a day like toothpaste like K-Y jelly to lubricate all the things you live through good and bad until the memories ah memories are like treasures you want to hear one?

Since you bought me a drink I guess I have to put out, the girl said. Talk away. God you are so corny.

Once said toastmaster Jimmy once when we were kids my mother took Gloria and me down to Tijuana to get our teeth filled because we both had cavities and the dentists were cheaper down there, so we got our fillings which I remember as clear as if someone had told me the whole story just last week and then we drove back to the border where there was a wait like there always is in life in love in hospitals and it was so hot in the car since my mother made us keep the windows up (I think she was kind of nervous about some Mexican ramming into her for the insurance because I can remember her honking the horn every minute looking back and forth like a trapped rat not daring to turn off the motor and all the time telling us to be quiet and shaking her head *no* real fast if some Mexican kid knocked on the windshield trying to sell flowers or clean the windshield) anyhow we sat there in the heat for hours it seemed so Gloria and I got restless as kids will you know like kids smashing bottles on the sidewalk not that we were bad kids said Jimmy as the girl stirred her drink as if the fate of the world depended on an absolutely even distribution of ice cubes so said Jimmy when this Mexican came by yelling *chiclets! chiclets!* or however you say it he meant gum Gloria and I both started whining until my mother got brave or desperate enough to roll down her window and buy us some, then I remember how happy Gloria and I were, sitting together as close as you and me right now and Jimmy slid his hand into the girl's lap and she just looked at it until he took it away chewing our gum said Jimmy while a Mexican boy ran up and cleaned the windshield for a quarter even though my mother kept

shaking her head no . . . well that gum tasted as good as
Gloria's kisses and I can taste it now that taste of happiness
babe you should have seen us blowing bubbles arguing over
who could blow the biggest—and then all the sudden our
fillings popped out! So after all that wait we had to go back
to the dentist's. But on the way there Gloria and I mixed up
the fillings in the gum so I'd have some of hers and she'd
have some of mine and it always makes me feel good to know
that I have some of Gloria's fillings in my mouth.

That story was *so* sweet I think I'm going to puke, sneered
the ungrateful girl, at which Jimmy frowned and started to
wonder how much longer to put up with her and he wondered
also whether her sadness were as plain, as honest as a fat
whore spread-eagled against a brick wall or was it *phony* in
fact like a whore whose face was so powdered and wigged
that she was like a smooth white plastic doll with plastic black
hair and plastic earrings and plastic white teeth that matched
her new white dress and just above her crotch a plastic ruby
glittered as she stood against the wall so happily and the
headlights of cars pitched by like gobs of napalm and it was
very dark.—The girl had hardly touched her drink although
the ice cubes were melting nicely.

It sounds kind of sappy I guess said Jimmy drinking his
fourth Budweiser which the bartender had popped down in
front of him at a single majestic incurve of Jimmy's finger
but without Gloria I wouldn't be anything wouldn't even
know myself.

I'm not sure how to put this said the girl very seriously so
that he liked her again but do you think some people are just
not meant to get loved? I mean you can try and try so hard
and it just never happens.

Oh *baby* don't *ever* think that or no one *will* love you you
gotta maintain a positive attitude stay in combat readiness
keep your eyes peeled especially a gal as beautiful as you
shouldn't have any trouble why my friend Dinah (she's not
half as beautiful as you) she gets all the dates she wants so

78

just keep your chin up and keep LOOKING yes said Jimmy from his vantage point of solved universal problems like one of those brick hotels that looked down on the corner where Nicole used to stand holding to the fire alarm pole (but as Luna said Nicole had gotten stabbed) being in love Jimmy said is a beautiful feeling it makes me take big steps walk fast knowing the whole Tenderloin belongs to me. I could go ANYWHERE because I'm master of all I survey.

If you have such a great relationship with your wife the girl pounced at last where's she now? And how come you wear old clothes and need a shave? And if you don't mind my saying so did you know that you could use a bath?

Well uh said Jimmy gripping the counter hard she's visiting with our friend Phyllis in the hospital who got kidnapped last week when she was waiting for the bus you see this bastard whom they haven't caught yet took her right across the Bay Bridge and onto the freeway you know way out of the territory and he said he was going to drive her up into the Orinda hills and rape her so she had to jump out of the car at sixty miles an hour and her face was cut open from *here* to *here* and she's been at SF General ever since. Gloria said I'm gonna get her a big bunch of roses I said get her some candy from me they say with plastic surgery she'll look as good as before, but you never know I mean that's the kind of thing they *always* say to make you feel better. Me, I don't trust doctors.

Why can't you be straight? the girl said. I don't care what your story is as long as it's straight.

Honey you OK? said Jimmy.

No, the girl said, and looking sharply at her Jimmy saw that her face was quivering like a disturbed pool of water whose reflected images keep shimmering and shaking like a girl about to cry. I'm sorry, she said. I can't help it I can't *help* it! Just leave me alone.

In that case, said Jimmy brightly, maybe I better go tidy up the place for Gloria before she gets back, but here's three bucks to buy yourself another drink and I do want you to know that I'm rooting for you and wish you all the best.

You and your Gloria, the girl said, make me so fucking sick.

15

The cave of sheets

Jimmy walked around all night admiring the whores and thinking how nice it would be to stick his tongue up their dirty asses oh—*oh*! but the unhappy girl had upset him with her weeping ways; it now seemed that he could never be tranquil anymore like the transparent greenness inside a nice fat bottle of Cutty Sark, with the surface of the whisky barely trembling so that you know that it is there and waiting for you to drink it and it is right in front of you and all you have to do is reach over half a foot and start unscrewing that navy-white cap with the clipper ship on it and Jimmy had once counted all the sails on that ship let's see in his mind's eye a bank of four and two banks of five big ones each but Jimmy rarely drank Cutty Sark anymore because it was not that cheap a drunk. So maybe Code Six was right, and Jimmy did need to escalate it a little farther. He saw a pair of dirty panties on Larkin Street, but they were not good enough; he had to buy them from a whore to make them pure. In his dreams of Gloria he was hammering at Being, hammering at lightness to shape someone who would not turn her face away from him the way the whores he flatbacked did; she had to have a shape; he could no longer bear a glowing white facelessness for a face no matter how holy it was; he had to have Gloria and Gloria had to be comfortable with all her things around her—not as many as Imelda Marcos's shoes, but enough to make her feel at home. But even this late (it should be said) Jimmy still knew that he was pretending like Phyllis pretended with a pretty wig whose locks half hid lips pouted into a heart, with false eyelashes meticulously applied, with the same care that an entomologist might apply to re-assembling the legs of some rare and brittle millipede that he hoards inside his cabinet of types, and he remembered how Melissa had said to him well one of the things I used to do to combat that boredom was building forts, building like a little cave with the sheets, crawling under it, like a little tent I was inside by myself, setting up housekeeping, just pretending I was somewhere else. It was kind of easy in that dark environment. That's what being a kid is about, pretending. You've got to pretend you're this, pretend you're that, pretend you're a grownup, pretend you're not, pretend you're somebody else. —That's right Melissa, sighed Jimmy to himself sitting on his bed, and when you're a grownup you've got to pretend you're *with* somebody else. What a lot of work and trouble everything is.

The questions

Gloria, are you still crying? I guess you're just doing what you've got to, but I wonder if happiness is growing inside you? Is it going to be a boy or a girl? A girl I guess because all the whores were girls. I'm just trying to understand you Gloria but it's so hard. I'm doing what I can. If I love you hard enough will I be able to see you? How many more happy stories do I have to hear because they're sticking to me like mud and making me walk more and more heavy so I need to know how many? How many? Gloria, do you understand what I'm saying? Gloria, I never stop thinking about you.

16

Peggy and Classic

When he met old Peggy ten nights later on the corner of
Ellis and Jones, his SSI check cashed by kindly Pearl, he
could tell just by looking at her that she was a shooter, though
whether she shot coke or smack he couldn't say, nor was it
really his business out here among the dark dirty old buildings that must have been nice once before he was born. —
Jimmy was glowing with power. He was *Homo erectus*. Tonight
he said to himself *tonight* I'm gonna GET Gloria I'm gonna
have her once and for all because I've heard so many stories
that I'm almost there and one more batch will get me there
kissing her fingers like cloud-fingers rolling over the Tenderloin at sunset and I'll love her because no matter what that
bitch at the Coral Sea said Gloria is and will be my wife.
My *wife*! I can taste her all around me so I know she's in me
I'm in her and we'll be together soon as that old whore starts
talking she looks like a talker and I have money so what more
can I say what more do I need?

Peggy was combing her stringy greasy hair and talking to
a younger prettier whore whom Jimmy knew as Classic *whatever* her real name was (Jimmy believed that whores were like
other actresses and deserved to have the glamor of their stage
names respected), and Classic wore a button saying PRICE
IS THE ONLY DIFFERENCE and now Peggy was sitting
like a grinning frog on the hood of the Lincoln that Jimmy
and Code Six liked (so someone had moved it from Larkin
Street; so someone owned it and might even care about it;
imagine that), and her T-shirt was hiked up to show her fat
smooth thighs, and her face was dirty with the rupture of so

many little veins, and she was leaning back on her blotchy arms to make her breasts stick out, and her long black hair streamed down her shoulders. Peggy always combed her hair. She couldn't help the way that her face looked anymore but the least she could do for her self-respect was to keep her hair nice. She was also proud of her white white teeth which matched the whites of her eyes as she sat beaming at the traffic with crossed legs and looking so carefree as if she had time and time but of course when men rented her her meter began running; that was how she survived.—When Jimmy wandered up to them and said how ya doin' girls sure is a lovely night with YOU in it even if it *is* foggy and chilly and windy! it was Classic who turned to face him with the calm assumption that he must want *her* because *she* was the pretty one; as for Peggy, being as Jimmy had already noted a shooter and therefore so sad and weak-worn and grimy in face and form and fingernails, she was so used to being passed over that she didn't even bother to glance at him but Jimmy just stepped closer and closer to Peggy until his shadow fell across her face and then she looked up and when she breathed the skin contracted in her skinny throat and the corners of her mouth twitched and Jimmy grinned and then Peggy understood at last that he was interested. Classic had already hopped into a man's car. As she rode away, Jimmy saw her smiling at the driver and her lips were moving very fast and she was brushing her hair around her face to make the moment even more romantic, but she kept one hand on the door handle.

You know a safe place? said Jimmy.

This alley's pretty good, Peggy said. The only thing I ever touch though is a rubber. I don't give no head without a rubber. I don't fuck without a rubber. I had a guy offer five hundred dollars for a date and I told him sorry that doesn't cover my health.

I'll just stick it in you real quick, said Jimmy, and afterward you can tell me stories.

OK but you gotta give me the money first. Don't worry; I'm honest.

If you're not I'll just blow my brains out, laughed Jimmy.

Oh don't do that, said Peggy, bored. Too many people ahead of you. You gotta stand in line to do that.

Jimmy put his arm around her and she suffered that and they went into the alley and Jimmy thought she was going to take him between two cars but they walked around the corner and there were three pimps or dealers sitting on the steps by the garbage can and Peggy said to them would you mind taking a little walk while I do my business? When they left, Peggy pulled her dress up above her waist and knelt down in the filth of the street and stuck her ass out with her cunt bulging down beneath it as if only its matted and sticky hair kept it from bursting out from between her legs; that stinking bush of hers really resembled a black spider lurking there and clinging there, and Peggy's legs were covered with dark ovals and boils and there were scabby bumps on them as satisfying to the touch as the pleasure-dots on a french tickler, the sorii on a fern-leaf, and Peggy raised her ass high and dry to make it easy for Jimmy to get into her cunt and she buried her face in her crossed arms on the highest step. A Vietnamese boy watched out the window.

Jimmy said to himself Gloria must be with her somewhere although I don't see her; I just have to keep looking for her oh Gloria Gloria.

When he was done Peggy wiped herself and said are you married?

Yes, said Jimmy.

A lot of men are married, Peggy said, letting her dress fall back down her legs. They just need a little satisfaction. So I can honestly say that I've brought some marriages together.

Jimmy said well honey tell me some happy stories.

Peggy said I don't know any.

Fine Jimmy said then I want you to tell me stories about

things that happened to you and things you expect to happen to you in the future.

OK, said Peggy. But I don't want no one to see me just talking like this. They'll think I'm a snitch.

Well then keep your eyes about you, Jimmy said. And move over just a little because there's another lady here although you can't see her and she wants to sit down, too.

Whatever, said Peggy.

Get to it.

I came to the city before college, said Peggy, did two years of college, got a real good job, job went bankrupt day before Christmas. As you know, I'm a white girl in the Tenderloin, so there ain't no cause for me to be broke. So I came up here on the hill and made real good money on my first day. I worked all day without pulling my pants down, so that was OK, 'cause I was pretty nervous, wondering if they was on the up and up. It was mostly blow jobs. I always made sure I was in the front seat, where I could have my hand on the handle and jump out if I needed to.

One time I was standing on Geary and Jones and I don't usually date black men but it was pretty hot out policewise and so I made an exception. Black guy drives up in a nice car, looks pretty proper, he's got a briefcase in the back seat. That's what we check for—what kinda business he might be in. And another thing I don't like is anybody taking me past Market Street. That's too far out of the territory. I allowed him to do that. He took me to this empty truck stop and he kept fondling my hair; he kept saying he had a fetish for my hair. Asked me to put my hair in a ponytail. So I put my hair in a ponytail, 'cause you know some people get kinda kinky, and so then he talked me into sitting in the back seat, how much more comfortable that would be. I was still a little leery of sitting in the back seat. If you're scared of me he says I'll take you back no problem. I really needed the money. You know, I'm out here on a day to day basis, never know where I'm gonna sleep, so I don't sleep with anybody for free. You know I gotta make sure I have the cash in my pocket. So I let him talk me into goin' ahead and gettin' in the back seat. So he tells me to turn my back to him, 'cause he wants to massage my shoulders and play with my ponytail. So I turn around. First thing he does is grab my ponytail and yank me down in the seat. Soon as I hit that seat I looked at him and said that sucks; somehow I knew this was gonna happen. He says all you got to do is cooperate I won't hurt you and he says I want you to take off your pants. I took off my pants. I was pretty shook by now; I was like in tears, 'cause I didn't know like *what* he was gonna do. You know, all the time we'd been drivin' there he kept the conversation goin' like he was a real nice guy. He really snowed me. He yanked me, and I knew that he was gonna rape me. I asked him would you *please* wear a rubber with me I said I'll cooperate I'll work with you I'll make sure that you're gonna get a good piece of ass to be honestly truthful. He says hey I'm into safe sex that's OK. So he put the rubber on and proceeded to rape me; it didn't last long at all; and he asked me to throw my clothes out of the car. I said no I'm not gonna do that I just can't do that. I was afraid he was gonna drive me down the road some, let me out naked. So when I refused I guess he realized OK she gave me a good job she did what I told her to do everything was cool, so he let me get out right then and there. He had his car pointed to the direction he needed to go. He'd backed in. So I got out and he just spun away to where I couldn't get his license plate number. That was one of my scariest moments, 'cause this was really humiliating. And so I had to walk miles back. My man at that time was in the pen for parole violation, and so I really didn't have any backup. Nobody knew what car I got in; nobody knew what kinda danger I mighta been in. I asked around, and he's done it quite a few times with women who have ponytails.

Gloria

He was so close to Peggy now and he could see the dirty wrinkles that went all the way around her neck in a tree-bark pattern and he could see the little black sore on her chin and the veins on her eyes but he also saw the fine profile of face that she still had and the hair she took such pride in and the soft look in her eyes as she sat remembering because even if most things hadn't been happy at least they were *her* memories and someone else wanted her to share them with him—why, it didn't matter. So Jimmy sat and listened thinking she's a good woman with a lot in her and as soon as he had thought this there seemed to him to be a majestic echoing hollowness to the things she said as if there were caverns and caverns inside her and then his heart began pounding because he thought there must be room then for you-know-who.

He felt a sense of delicious expectation, the anticipation of a chemist almost at the end of a long sequence, when the colorless liquids may at last be mixed and begin to blush with color, slowly but steadily brightening now like an annunciation, like someone you love coming, like Gloria becoming visible to his open eyes as he tasted her presence near him and he felt her unbearably close beside him and about to come into being out of love for him and then she was real and she sat between him and Peggy smiling and listening and she was both brighter and less transparent than he remembered from those dreamy sleepless nights in the Hotel Bailey when he had to look for her even when he was seeing her because he could not see her except through his faith in her but the faith was there knowing that she would get brighter, that someday she would have weight in his arms as well as softness, and now it had happened, so that of Peggy he could scarcely make out more than a silhouette with a hypothetical face-texture whose features were dirty and crumbling anyhow like the clay people that he and Gloria used to make at the river but he could see very clearly the bumps and scars on Peggy's naked legs because Peggy sat with them drawn in high because it was cold while Gloria let her legs dangle down to the concrete so that Peggy's legs were not obscured by Gloria and her light; and he could see more of Gloria's face than he had ever been able to see before and Peggy's stories seemed to be getting murkier and muddier like Peggy herself since they were going straight into Gloria's ears and becoming part of Gloria, part of who Gloria was and had always been, and Gloria was smiling and smiling and he could see the delicate pulse in her neck and her perfume smelled so fresh to him and her hair was so soft and silky to his touch and Peggy said oh are you one of those who like my hair too? and Jimmy said something and Peggy was saying something but Jimmy couldn't even see her anymore because Gloria was growing into her strength so quickly now that it was happening before his eyes while the memories flashed and glowed like Melissa's afternoon movies to light up the darkness that he sat in which became darker and vaster and more and more forgotten, and he saw Gloria brushing her hair back from her face and talking very rapidly and he could see her lips move but he could not quite hear what she said; he was driving her home to the flat they had together on Pacific Avenue where the houses were immaculate and Peggy said are you all right? and Jimmy said keep talking and tall trees shaded the sidewalk and Jimmy slept well at night because the neighbors were quiet older people who kept the blinds drawn and rarely came out except to wash their cars. Schoolchildren waited at the bus stop, and the buses rolled slowly past the blue and white houses in silence, and there was a view of the ocean from the top of the hill at Pacific and Lyon where Jimmy and Gloria sometimes walked in the evenings when he got back from work (Gloria usually finished her job about half an hour earlier because she worked straight through lunch) and on Saturdays they went to one of the parks and had a picnic with salami and cheese and pickles and French bread and the grass was warm and wet to the touch and children chattered like squirrels and men and women snuggled on pretty blankets and Gloria scratched her knee sleepily and said darling would you like a beer and Jimmy said no I don't think I'll drink today how about passing me a seltzer and Gloria said what a good boy and her long hair trembled in the sunny breeze and Jimmy said you know babe I really have a thing for your hair and Gloria said that's sweet even if you do always say that and Jimmy said I'd love it so much if you'd put your hair in a ponytail for me and Gloria said why a ponytail? and Jimmy said remember how you wore it braided in a ponytail when we were kids and we took that train ride? and Gloria laughed and said of *course* I remember I remember everything about that trip although I was even littler than you and the windows were so high above my head that I had to stand on Mother's lap to see the snowflakes coming down outside and all the grownups seemed as tall as redwood trees do you remember that part of it? and Jimmy said yes and Gloria said but you know hon I remember something sad about that trip too I remember how in Louisiana they had separate bathrooms for white and colored why honey you've gone pale did I say something to upset you? but Jimmy said you don't remember that part correctly nothing bad like that happened I think you must have just read about it in the schoolbooks anyway not to change the subject how about putting your pretty hair in a ponytail for your man? and Gloria said if that's what you want Jimmy and began putting her hair up and gathering it and Jimmy said oh darling you look just like the little girl I remember now turn your back to me and let me rub your shoulders and when Gloria couldn't see what he was doing anymore he took her ponytail in both hands and

and Gloria said let's go downtown and they went into a bakery where the cakes were covered with flowers of frosting

90

and there were loaves of pumpkin bread heavy with raisins and the sugar cookies glittered like stars and Gloria got a chocolate éclair and when she was done Jimmy kissed the frosting off her lips.

Peggy

One time said Peggy I picked up this *real* nice, clean-cut man, but he was *built*, really built good. I got him up into my motel room and he told me he was a hit man. He *murdered* people for a living. All he wanted to do was talk. When he told me his profession I thought, *mmmarvelous!* the things I get myself into, right? All he wanted to do was talk about the people he killed, how sorry he was that he had to do it, but it *was* his job. He told me a few little details, an' I was really on pins and needles.

Not my kind of work, said Jimmy. Did he look in their faces when he killed 'em?

Yeah. He looked 'em *dead* in their eyes, as he's lookin' *dead* in my eyes. Now the man's armed, so I was pretty shook up. But I acted real calm and I kept the conversation goin', and that's just about all you really need to do to keep your safety. Never let them know that you're gonna panic or you don't want their company—and he had *paid* me for that half-hour that he wanted to talk. That really tripped me out when somebody knocked on the door. He jumped up off the bed drew his gun I didn't know if he was gonna put *rounds* in it or what. I said sit down an' *relax*, whoever's at my door I'm not gonna open it, just gonna tell them through the door that I'm busy and to get on. So I did that, but I mean that was a real spooky experience.

Gloria

Gloria was sitting very still on the steps, and for a moment Jimmy thought that what Peggy had said had paled her and diminished her, but she smiled at him over her shoulder and he saw that she had not been hurt, that she had known that these were not her memories, and for the first time he could see her eyes very clearly; they were like Melissa's eyes; and he hugged her and said good girl way to go babe don't be afraid because you know those kind of men don't even *exist* and Peggy said what the hell are you talking about and Jimmy said hey I paid you didn't I so just keep on talking.

Peggy

Just recently said Peggy I had aggravated a gentleman who'd just murdered someone down the street. It didn't make me feel too good. He was very much pussy-whipped, OK? His old lady just ran the whole show and yet she wasn't doin' *shit*. I'm very honest; I walked up an' I confronted him about it. He slapped me. I said well that's what you felt you needed to do but my opinion stands. Meanwhile everyone's pulling me away trying to walk me off, saying that this man will stab you in the back when you aren't looking; don't aggravate him. So OK fine. I left it at that. Not more than two days after that he had murdered his girlfriend's trick. Girlfriend's got a real hard time getting dates. I don't know she's just not aggressive enough she's just real stupid. Apparently she got a date took the date up to her room then Blackwell popped out of the closet and stabbed him, killed him. So now he's on the run an' I don't have to worry about him no more.

Gloria

No Jimmy it's OK, Gloria said, I didn't drink that story, either. And I don't even need many more stories because what I see and remember is already making me what I am.

Her fingernails now came into being, one by one, sparkling with the newness of diamonds.

Peggy

I had a date just last week with a black man, said Peggy. He picked me up asked me if I was clean I told him yes I'm clean only because I use rubbers and I see my doctor *faithfully* and he says well I don't know about the rubber part I says well if you want to date me that's what you have to do, so he accepts this. And meanwhile he's just asking me questions; you can tell if you're being interrogated. He takes me to the Sunset Inn over on Van Ness and we go up to his room. It's like 1776 or something; I don't *think* I'd forget his room number. But when I got in there he laid out all his jewelry, so it was kind of a setup to me; I don't steal from my dates. He was putting things where if I were a thief I would've taken them. I said you know I really have a funny feeling that you don't *want* a date are you gonna hurt me? — If you don't put me in that position he says I won't hurt you. — So I says look I can give you your money back there's no problem here. I can walk home or something. I really don't need this date to the point where I'm gonna get hurt if that's what it's gonna take to satisfy you. He says you know I just want some head and if you're good enough you're not gonna get hurt. Well luckily I'm real good at that. But all the time I was servicing him I was in fear. So when I finished servicing him yeah I could tell that he was checking out where his diamond rings and things were, so I didn't get nowhere *near* 'em, so

I says are you done with me now he says *yes* I'm *done* here's a dollar for bus fare. Well I'm not gonna argue with him I'm not gonna say *oh*, you're not gonna bring me back? I didn't do that. I was pretty shook to where I just walked. You know I'm a pretty good judge of character and you really have to watch out the look they have and the way they drool.

Gloria

Jimmy looked at Gloria again and she cast a shadow now and her flesh had the firmness of flesh; she was completely opaque to the streetlights now, and he understood that when he got up to leave she would walk away with him and be visible beside him forever, and a tremendous pride and excitement pounded in his heart. He knew that she knew all that he had done to clothe and adorn her with memories. He could see her jewelry now; she was becoming that substantial, with the necklace and bracelets and earrings that he had given her that time when he had gotten through the probationary period on his job and the boss looked him *dead* in the eye and told him Jimmy not only are we going to keep you but we like your work so much we're gonna give you a raise and Jimmy went down to the jewelry store after work and bought rings and bracelets and pearl earrings and scattered them all over the bedroom in little boxes with bows and ribbons and Gloria's eyes got so big when she got home and Jimmy said they're all for you babe and Gloria said but but but where did you get the money? and Jimmy told her and Gloria clapped her hands and rushed around opening her presents hugging him and saying Jimmy you're the best oh look at this oh look how this one sparkles oh Jimmy thank you I love you so I'll never ever leave you. — Gloria made love to him wearing her jewelry and then she arranged it all around the bed where they lay together and the alarm clock was softly ticking and Gloria's face was ever so faintly luminous and Gloria said oh you're so warm, so warm, and Jimmy rubbed her shoulders and Gloria said your skin feels nice and their bodies rested against each other as they were meant to and Jimmy lay watching Gloria sleep and he saw that the second hand of his watch was broken and then he yawned and laid down his head on her shoulder and went to sleep.

But all that had happened long ago because Jimmy did not *need* it to happen anymore; Gloria was real and finished.

Well Peggy said Jimmy nice talking to you.

At home

He came into the lobby and paid his rent to Pearl and went up the stairs not yet acting as if Gloria were with him (even though she was) for the same reason that at the Black Rose it was taboo to change a wig in public; one always did it in the bathroom; for the same reason that women don't show their cunts to everybody, which is why there are whores . . . and Jimmy fell down onto his bed with Gloria beside him and Gloria said I want to move out of here tomorrow and Jimmy said whatever you want, you know I'll do it and she smiled and said I know and he said it does kind of get you here the first time although I forgot that and she said tomorrow we'll start getting used to another place and he said you'll tell me where, won't you? and she said oh come on Jimmy don't be afraid; pretty soon you and I will be living in a nice house and he said it's just that I feel so tired and rested his head on the fluffy pillows that soon became a feast of mashed potatoes covered with the thin brown gravy of dreams.

17

Perpetual motion

The next morning Gloria was gone, and Jimmy said well shit I guess I gotta go hear more stories or do something different get real things to anchor her to earth like more hair from Dinah or something like that I don't know.

The truth is, he admitted to himself, I forgot about her for a minute, just like with that cunt Nicole that hurried me up on the kitchen floor!

She came in with me and then I pretended she wasn't there when I paid the rent to Pearl so Pearl wouldn't charge us double and then she was with me on the stairs and I got into bed and yes that's when I forgot her.

She was almost there for real and I forgot her. She got away from me. No sense even calling to her. She's so far away right now she couldn't even hear me.

Jimmy was very downcast. He knew life was going to get worse. Maybe stories aren't enough, he thought. But no; they *have* to be. Stories and hair.

18

Being misconstrued

The night that Jimmy cashed his next SSI check he went out past the brick hotels whose deep-set windows were shaded and curtained so that nobody could see which pair of desperate old eyes peered fiercely out, and fire escapes made Z's upon Z's.

The whore whose stockings were flowers and holes peered fishily at him through her glasses. I heard about you, she said. I'm not letting you shave *my* pussy.

That's not the kind of hair I want, Jimmy explained patiently. From your head'll work just fine.

Bet you wanna shave my armpits, too, she jeered. Dontcha? Dontcha?

It was so late that it was almost morning, and the nightlights were dead behind barred basement windows and he was tired; he was so tired of pretty girls and their cunts. He did not want to fuck them anymore. Their tits seemed almost as stupid as his cock. He remembered how when he was younger every pretty girl had made him hard, and then later he lusted after pretty girls without getting hard, and later he just enjoyed looking at them, and later he didn't enjoy looking at them so much.

Do you believe in Gloria? he asked her, straight out.

Gloria? Who the *fuck* is that?

Sometimes I don't believe in her either, he admitted. Sometimes I don't believe in anything except not believing. — He spat on the sidewalk and winked. He scratched the fly of his pants. — But if seeing is believing, he went on, then I sure better believe *my* eyes because here you are *right* in

front of me unless looks are deceiving, which I'm not sayin'
they are and I'm not sayin' they aren't, and you are a *sight*
to see baby I'm *telling* you you are fucking HOT! How about
it, huh? Let me kiss your lips (you *know* which ones!). How
about it?

Drop dead, said the whore.

Dinah

Well *hey* Dinah said Jimmy welcome back from jail. You back
at the Hotel Cheyenne?

Listen said Dinah fiercely I am so pissed off at you! You
been telling everyone you're jerking off in that hair I let you
cut off. I never should have let you do it, you pervert. Jack
says he'll cut you if he ever sees you on the street again.

I never said that to anyone Dinah, said Jimmy, so don't
go and have a period about it. Who told you that anyway?

Pearl.

Pearl told you that?

Oh cut it said Dinah just cut it.

Listen, Dinah, uh Pearl's a little jealous of my wife Gloria
I guess she's well she's making up stories to get me in trouble.
The truth is that Gloria needs more hair she's balder than
a baby's crotch and if you give me your new address so I can
come and get more hair I'm sure I can make you very happy
Dinah if you know what I mean.

So what are you saying to me? said Dinah, clenching her
fists.

Tell me your new address.

Give me five dollars! Dinah shouted.

No, said Jimmy.

Then *fuck* my address I don't live anywhere anyway I don't
have a place to stay tonight so *fuck* it.

OK said Jimmy well if you ever want to get in touch with me I might have more money to give you then.

When'll you be down here on Jones Street? said Dinah.

Every day. Today's Monday. I'll be here Tuesday, and I'll be here Wednesday.

I'll be talking to you, said Dinah, stalking up the street. And so will Jack.

Classic

There was Classic stretched out on the hood of Code Six's Lincoln; her pretty ass had polished the dust away. She lay with her fingers splayed, gazing at him from behind her shoulder. But her pride was never to tell anyone anything. That was how she kept her privacy. — Fine with me, Jimmy thought, but that means Gloria and I can't use you. And Gloria can't use me and I can't use me so . . . So what. — He started walking on. — Oh how she threw back her shoulders like flames with burning breasts lips eyes igniting him — and yet the light from her was just the same streetlight that glittered indifferently on her earrings. — What do I need you for? Jimmy thought sourly. The same light falls on me, too. You don't have a monopoly on it.

Where you goin'? sobbed Classic. How come you never want me?

Sure I'd like to stick it in you, said Jimmy gallantly. But the truth is that I'm faithful. You may not think so, but my business is my business. I don't have to justify myself.

She tried to smile. But she was shivering, even though it was a hot night.

Jimmy hitched his thumbs in the loops of his jeans. — Need your fix? he said. Is that why you're doing the Jello act?

Her eyes dropped. Can I borrow five? she said. I need to, really bad.

Need's what it's all about out here, isn't it, girl? Maybe I need it just as much as you.

She didn't say anything, and he walked on into the darkness, humming Gloria Gloria, but then he was ashamed of himself and went back and stuck a dollar into her hand.

Jack

What you did to my woman is kind of an insult, said Jack. She's feeling pretty bad about it.

Is that a fact? said Jimmy, swishing his tongue around in his mouth.

Yes that *is* a fact and it's not going to be easy to make things right with her, said Jack. Dinah's kind of got a bug up her ass about it.

Not the only thing she's had up her ass, now, is it, Jack? said Jimmy. Seems to me last time I saw you you told me to live long and prosper. Or was it the time before that?

So this is the way you want to have it? said Jack.

You know you're working yourself up over nothing, said Jimmy. If you want to fight, I'll fight. Is that what you want?

So that's how you want it, said Jack, looking Jimmy up and down. Then he walked away.

Jimmy knew that he had won. But he was shaking.

The Nitecap

How much did I drink in here last time? said Jimmy.

A lot, said the ugly barmaid.

Wow, said Jimmy, you're BEAUTIFUL. Well, I'm going to drink *twice* as much this time.

Dinah came up to her lamppost. She looked in the window and stuck her tongue out at him.

Jimmy drank and drank. He figured that if Gloria were gone he might as well do whatever he wanted. If he couldn't be happy-drunk he might as well be stupid-drunk. Then he was going to go out and fuck a whore and not think of Gloria at all.

Gloria

. . . And leaning against the marble wall of a hotel which had once been fancy, she pulled down the straps of her top to show her hellishly beautiful breasts as she ducked her head down giggling at him shyly raising one arm as if she were afraid of him (and on that arm he saw a long red scar running the length of the vein), and a streetlamp powdered her naked-ness very white and the cock of her mouth was very girlish because the wrinkles of age that she had planted around her lips had not yet taken deep root so she made her magic for him of naughty brown eyes and imitation turtleshell ear-rings which she had borrowed from Luna who said with contemptuous kindness take 'em and welcome, you poor old stinkbag and as she fixed her huge pupils on him she was not even thinking about money for the moment but the thrill of making him see her as she wanted to be for all these lonely men whose greed of lust was nothing but an aching prayer for beauty but then he shuffled a little and she thought oh please don't get away from me you sonofabitch I'll cross my legs around your balls to keep you because I need my fix so bad so bad.

Jimmy saw her eyes shining hugely at him and said why, that's what *my* eyes look like! I never would have thought it.

Are you dating or arentcha? said the whore.

Well, said Jimmy slowly, I'm sorry, but I just don't like the look of your eyes.

Gloria

Past an empty stretch of white wall with stone flowers inset below windows, he spied a pair of popeyed pimp-eyes as urgent as whore-eyes but roundly comical as the pimp twisted himself from side to side not to be sexy but to be *urgent* as if to say Jimmy this is your one and ONLY chance to get the woman whose cunt will satisfy you for ever and ever, in sickness and in health, so help me God, but you have to come with me right now down this dark dark alley past the sign that says MOVIES and left by the trash cans following the luminescence of my white straw hat and white jeans and the whites of my eyes which I will continually turn back upon you to make sure that you stay with me all the way to the barred basement windows where your good fortune waits for you already saying oh Jimmy Jimmy but as soon as the man opened his mouth he became as monotonous as the intricacies of brick walls and the steel lattice-windows of bars, and Jimmy walked away.

It was a chilly rainy evening. He passed a Sphinx-wise transvestite whose goose-pimpled thighs were gartered to black stockings so frilly that they must really let the wind in. On Grove Street, the men leaned against streetlamps watching girls. One of them said if I have on my new duds, I be *gaming* them tender, tender ittie-bitties! — He licked his lips, and saliva ran down his chin. Jimmy said to himself am I a dirty thing? Are these men dirty? Why were they made that way? Fuck it. I'm going home to jerk off.

19

The Black Rose

This time Jimmy sat directly in front of that purple-glowing black rose, beneath which was the point of it all, the cash register adorned with its purple Budweiser icon, and he ordered a Budweiser and sat waiting for Cecily, who was off duty until six but was supposed to meet him here at five because it had occurred to him that Cecily was not only soft and loving but also might have wonderfully happy stories to tell him because if he heard enough happy stories and put them in his *own* memory-bank then maybe he wouldn't need Gloria anymore. Gloria didn't want him? Fine. Anyhow the bitch was as phony as Dinah's party smile. But he had to pull himself together fast. That whore turning him down and the whore with the eyes and Jack and Dinah added up to something no good like the pregnant snaggletooth girl in the Coral Sea who kept looking at him grinning while her boy-friend in the coontail cap kept whispering into her ear and Jimmy felt a kick of panic. So maybe Cecily could present to him the facts of comfort. He remembered how once an old man had drunk too much and Cecily said to him baby you shouldn't have no more and the old man swore and started wobbling out the door and Cecily said can I call you a cab? and he said no I can make it on my own two fucking pins thank you and he squeezed through that heavy door like a bug emerging from an almost-closed desk drawer and he took a step outside and another and fell and smashed his head open on the sidewalk so Cecily took him to the hospital and went down again an hour later to check on him and Jimmy thought what a loving person she does care and she must know secret good things about the whores that make memories worthy of Gloria, and she has nice hair too she is *so* sexy (although he sometimes wanted almost to weep for her not that *he* ever cried because in spite of all her femininity she must remain a big tall girl, having the bones of men; she had a man's hairy arms, and even if she were to award herself the Christmas prize, the star, the transsexual's vagina clean and pure, it would find itself living between a man's great thighs) so he bought a bottle of fancy wine at the liquor store and left it with Regina to give to Cecily but when he saw Cecily the next day and she said softly hey baby and he asked her if she'd gotten it, she said ohh that was so thoughtful of you thank you so much but someone stole it and I know who and they're coming in tonight and believe me I will speak to them I will get my *revenge* and it was then that Jimmy made the appointment for five the next day at the Black Rose and Cecily promised that she'd be there, but she never showed. So he sat there, morose, and had another beer and felt a vague increep of energy but not enough to compensate for the swelling in his head, and a whore beside him said angrily to him *oh* you're *listening* to our conversation that's *not* cute, and Jimmy, who still had Cecily and therefore Gloria on his mind, said wearily hi what's your name, and the whore said Sugar and Sugar did not ask Jimmy who he was but she did say honey you know I could use a drink you know apples and oranges and Jimmy didn't say anything and Sugar ordered her drink and just before it came she wandered to the jukebox and Regina said well Jimmy I take it you're paying for this and Jimmy said that's news to me and Regina slid the drink to the man on the other side of Sugar's empty stool and said well how about you and the man glared at Jimmy saying I'd be *honored* to pay for it and when Sugar returned he said to him *honey* I am *honored* to make your acquaintance.

Whoop-de-doo, said Jimmy.

Just then a lady came sliding onto the stool just left of

Jimmy's and said *well* it's my favorite drinker and Jimmy looked at her with her big dark handsome face and her sweet eyes and thought I must have seen her before I think I saw her before maybe she's Linda who used to live with Phyllis before she got busted, although he was far from a hundred per cent sure, but the lady was looking at him so he said well Beautiful what a *nice* dress and how have you been? and she said smiling sadly oh I've been fine and she said did that guy with you on the motorcycle ever get his money back? and Jimmy said no but I think he was just too drunk to know he'd spent the money I don't think Phyllis would do that and the lady said I *know* Phyllis would do it and Jimmy said are you still living in the Hotel Canada? and the lady said don't you know who I am I'm Luna! and now Jimmy remembered that evening with Luna and her black face and her embracing him and him embracing her and he said well sure Luna of course I remember you sorry to get you mixed up and Luna looked down at the floor and Luna said in his ear listen baby come with me to my hotel room on Van Ness and I'll tell you stories and give you such a good *massage* and Jimmy had a funny feeling inside and said well that's awfully nice of you Luna but I don't have any money right now and Luna said softly you don't have to give me any money and Jimmy's jaw fell open — he had never heard such astonishing words in his life! — and he sat there for a minute and he said I hope you don't mind that I'm so quiet and Luna said that's OK I'm quiet too and Jimmy said those sure are *nice* sunglasses you have there Luna and Luna took them off and said here I'm giving them to you and Luna said I love you and Jimmy started feeling such guilt and pity and sadness for Luna and Jimmy said can I buy you a drink? and Luna bit her lip and said that'd be nice and Jimmy said what do you drink? and Luna said almost inaudibly tequila sunrise and Jimmy shouted hey Regina a tequila sunrise for Luna! and Regina said two-twenty-five and the cash register jinged and the disco ball sped its bubbles of light across the back wall and the light-blinks zipped crazily around the mirrors and ladies came in with hair like poodle-fur and Jimmy said well Luna a penny for your thoughts and Luna said I'm just thinking of you and Jimmy said well *thanks* Luna and after a long time Luna said well I guess I'll go sit over by the window.

Jimmy put Luna's sunglasses in his coat pocket, determined to keep them for ever. He felt horrible about the fact that Luna was not his type. But there was nothing that he could do about it. Later, on his way out, he went up to Luna alone at his little table and kissed him on the cheek.

Bye, Luna said. Tears rolled down his lovely face.

20

Melissa

Not long after that, Jimmy met Melissa again at the corner of Hyde and Turk, not far from the Hotel Tony where you had to pay old Lonnie three dollars to get in, and Melissa was looking good, so Jimmy said well how's it been going? and Melissa said ups and downs mostly downs and Jimmy said yeah well you know all the happy stories you told me were sad but I made them happy for myself just by showing myself dark cool movies of 'em like you used to do when you were a girl, and Melissa smiled and took his hand and said I'm glad now what was your name again?

Jimmy.

By the way Jimmy one thing I forgot to tell you is that once when I went to that movie house—I must have been about seven—I met a child molester and he kept sitting closer and closer to me and he told me I love the way you eat that hot dog and he told me to jerk him off.

Jimmy said no Melissa no don't say that it was perfect for Gloria the way it was please don't change it.

Gloria

What am I going to do? shouted Jimmy soundlessly, down inside his throat.

He went home and drank beer alone until he was calm.

The problem he said to himself is how can I put one foot ahead of the other day after day for the rest of my life?

Goddamn it! shouted Jimmy in the empty room. If she's not there what the hell am I supposed to do? I'm just trying to get by day after day. It used to be, if I wanted a Bud, I drank it. If some cunt walked by and I wanted her box, I bought it. Then I had something special that was changing me, and that was for the best. I never forgot about it. Just too bad it happens to be gone. Get it, Gloria? Get it? Hey, cunt, is my business still your business?

Gloria

That night went by, and so did the next. Jimmy didn't come out of his room except to piss and drink water from the bathroom sink. He heard nothing but silence. He said to himself everything grows out of something. Gloria must have grown out of something. If she's gone there must be something left. But I can't figure out what. —He lay on his bed with the light on until the bulb burned out and then it was dark and he lay there until Pearl was knocking on the door saying Jimmy? and he moaned something until she went away. Then that day was full and over, like a wastebasket full of beer bottles and used rubbers.

I guess you screwed me, all right, he said. Right up the butt.

Well, shit, he said. Things are pretty cheesey since you left. Maybe I'll just pretend you're here. And if I don't tell you won't tell. I have you figured there, don't I? Because if you tell you'll have to come back to do it.

He laughed and said to himself maybe I could use a beer.

21

Peggy

Well, sweetycakes, what kind of dreams exactly do you have? said Jimmy. I never have dreams so I'm gonna memorize yours if you don't mind which somehow I have the feeling you won't because here's five dollars.

Peggy breathed hard and said I had a nightmare just a few nights ago that I was in the stairway of a hotel. I'm running up and down on the stairway and I got these two guys clowning me. They're teasing me, and one's at the top of the steps and I'd run down and I'd run into the other one. I can't get away from 'em. And if they ever got close enough they'd start trying to take my clothes off. I kept looking for my man Titus, but I couldn't find him. He never came through to rescue me. He woke me up once, and I was too sleepy to really come out of it. Yeah, I couldn't get away from 'em. I lost two nights' sleep over it. I was afraid, really afraid.

Pearl

I had a bad dream last night, said Jimmy, thinking to himself my lies are so bad not even *I* believe 'em. He looked Pearl in the eye and locked his face into the loopy sincerity that she might believe before he said I dreamed that Gloria was trapped on the stairs between these two pimps who wanted to hurt her and they kept sorta playing with her by throwing jewels at her and telling her about all the people they'd stabbed and blown away and then they threw this dead German shepherd bitch at her and she saw they'd cut its cunt out and started calling to me like she was in real trouble, really afraid, and I could hear her through the wall but the door was locked and I couldn't find the key. Finally I broke down the door and rescued her.

That's good Jimmy, said Pearl. I'm real glad it ended happy.

Yeah, Jimmy said. But you know the funny thing was that these pimps were *women*! They looked like Black Rose types, big and tall but with kinda delicate faces like Luna or Regina, and I thought I'd seen them both before in the street somewhere. One of them had a ponytail, and the other one was kind of like Dinah—you know her, don't you, Pearl? The one that tells lies? They kept whispering these awful things, and every time they'd say something they'd throw a little dart at Gloria and it never missed her—pierced her and went right in her and she was bleeding and crying so every time one of those darts hit her she got thinner and paler until I could see right through her! What do you think that means? I can't figure it. Actually I don't remember much that they were whispering but one time they said Gloria you whore we're gonna take you to the movies. When I finally got there and they saw me they started laughing but I charged at 'em back and forth and they turned into big clay statues you know ceramic and I smashed 'em. But the main thing is I saved her I *saved* her.

Pearl cleared her throat. You know, Jimmy, she said, if Gloria ever doesn't work out for you I want you to know that I'm here.

Thanks Pearl said Jimmy, taking in all the honest ugliness of her, the bad breath and good nature and loving kindness of her, and then he paid his rent and went out.

110

Gloria

Well, I didn't do too bad that time did I? he laughed, leaning against a wall on Turk Street. I did pretty good considering I don't even believe in you.

He took a stroll down to Sixth Street, walking cocky, and heard Code Six puking in his alley and politely waited until the sounds stopped before he ambled in and said hey Code Six! How's life, buddy? You pulling through?

Damned straight I am, said Code Six. That's why Walgreen's sells Vaseline.

Gloria

Stories and hair he said to himself again on the bed that's the ticket, stories and hair. Just keep pretending, step by step, and then you're back around the block.

Fine.

What next?

22

Spider

Pleased to know ya, Jimmy said. He stuck out his hand.

Spider's handshake was cold and limp. Spider's wrist dangled down against Jimmy's fingers. Spider did not bother to look at Jimmy when he shook his hand.

Jumper and Boz told me to come to you, Jimmy said.

What do you want? said Spider. I assume you want something.

I hear you have all different kinds of girls, Jimmy said. Now see this hair in this matchbox this is my wife Gloria's hair do you have any girls with hair like that?

That's just reg'lar nigger hair, said Spider. Any one of my girls got hair like that.

Well I want more of it, Jimmy said. I've been in difficulties lately and I'm kind of floundering around, but I think if I get enough of it I may be able to start all over again. I want one of your girls to cut all her hair off to match this so I can make a wig out of it and then any whore I go with can wear it, you see what I'm saying?

You want one of my girls to be bald? said Spider. You trying to insult me? Listen you I grew up on the West Side of Chicago you know what that means?

It means a hundred bucks to you, Jimmy said.

Spider spat on the sidewalk, carefully, right between Jimmy's feet. Two hundred is what it means, he said.

Hey Spider I don't have that kind of money, said Jimmy, what do you think I am, Joe Million?

Everybody be Joe Million for two days when his check

come in. Now I be considerin' your proposal; I be cool and you be cool. You gimme some kinda *value* for my time.

Hundred twenty-five, said Jimmy.

Pay me now.

All right, I owe you, Jimmy said, swallowing. My check comes in this afternoon.

You mean you been wasting my time for *nothing*? said Spider. Is that what you're trying to say to me? I don't like that. I could *pawn* you. I could take you down to Turk Street and sell your ass. You want that?

I'll be coming down here tomorrow morning, said Jimmy. You have that bag of hair.

You tell me when, said Spider, and you tell me where, and you better *be* there or we're gonna have a real talk. You know I could easily take somethin' and just start hittin' you upside the head.

Yeah, Spider, we all have ways of defending ourselves, said Jimmy.

But when Spider heard this, he walked off as Jimmy was speaking and strode up the block to show his displeasure. Jimmy figured that he would be back, and here he came, just like a mosquito.—Now where it gonna be? he said.

The Black Rose, at twelve o'clock, said Jimmy. His throat was dry, and he knew that Spider knew that he was nervous. Spider liked to make people nervous.

That night Jimmy reclined on his bed, which was very sturdy and had withstood thirty years forty years of screwings beatings rapes and thrown dead weight; he rested the back of his neck against the headboard and stared down at his wriggling toes; he looked around him, looked into the closet where his spare shirt lay crumpled, look at the scratched-up desk beside him that served for bureau and night table with a wavering row of empty beer cans that he had not yet crushed, looked at the wastebasket with its moldy apple core and the mummy of an old tampon, stared up at the ceiling where the light bulb hurt his eyes, smelled the insecticide smell that grew simultaneously staler and more concentrated week by week when the exterminator came because Jimmy never opened the window to air the place out; and then there was nothing more to notice so Jimmy began to play with his keys. He felt very safe and happy to think that his door was double-locked, that downstairs in the lobby whose pillars and wide easy wall-curves proclaimed that it had once been plush Pearl sat in her little glass box keeping an eye on everything, and if anyone wanted to get in, he had to talk Pearl into buzzing him in. Outside, beneath the sign that said TRANSIENTS WELCOME, Spider leaned, hawking on the sidewalk, pulling the brim of his cap lower and lower over his eyes because he thought now I be lookin' MEAN! and wide pipes clambered up the wall of the hotel like vines and light glowed white and dim through the little window in the door up the steps behind the great steel grating that Spider might have clawed over inch by inch without finding a way in; and behind Spider stretched a flank of stucco wall studded with reflectors and then the Vietnamese vegetable market which was now closed and then parking meters and parked cars all the way to Code Six's Lincoln on the hood of which Luna lay sprawled barefoot in new white sneakers and she wore black jeans and a dazzling white California T-shirt and she smiled and waved at every passing car. A rattly old Dodge pulled up, and two men got out with baseball bats. Luna sat up abruptly. —You the fag that tried to pick my pocket? said one of the men.

But the next day Jimmy had his money; Pearl had cashed his check; and Spider was waiting on the corner saying my wife said you be late but I told her you still five minutes early you got my money?

Sure do, said Jimmy.

Spider smiled. Here's what you told me to get for you, he said. I cut it off my wife myself.

Snitches

At the corner of Turk and Jones the pushers were pushing and Jimmy went and leaned up against a building with them and watched the whores go by and a pusher said you want a bag? and Jimmy said no thanks I got a bag right here, a paper bag with treasure in it and the pusher said you ain't no cop I trust 'cause if you are you gonna be *dead* and Jimmy said no not me and another pusher came up to him and said what you doin' here and Jimmy said what's happening pal and the pusher said coldly pal's not my name and Jimmy said well I'm Jimmy pleased to meet you Charlie and he stretched out his hand and the pusher just looked at it and Jimmy said well if that's the way you want it and the pusher took a quart of beer out of a paper sack and smashed it down on the sidewalk so that it exploded and sprayed beer and broken glass all over the sidewalk and the pusher just kept looking at Jimmy in disgust saying *shit* and Jimmy said yep Charlie you can sure say *that* again.

He pulled out the wig he had bought from Spider and put it on and the pushers all said see I *told ya* he's a cop! and then they giggled and said oh no I guess he's just a fag I guess he's just another one of them Miss Things.

Jimmy said don't snitch on me boys I'm just a he-she and now let me hide this wig away and go get some ACTION.

You be *crazy*! the pushers laughed and laughed.

Jimmy strolled up to Ellis and Leavenworth and met the ugliest old whore he had ever seen in his life although thanks to Vaseline or whatever it was her lips glistened like the retro-shimmer of rockets. Here we have the Whore of Hell, he thought to himself: Abandon hope all ye who enter her. Listen baby, she told him, Wino Jimmy is an undercover Fed he snitched on the whole Tenderloin you see this steel comb I'm gonna go find him and carve his eyes out. — Good luck, Jimmy grinned.

115

Gloria

He was in a fine mood. His life was about to change. He had the treasure.

More decisions

So now as in the old days Jimmy also known as James went whore-hunting. And he said to himself I now make my harvest in the garden of black roses and coral sea anenomes and delicate little nightcap flowers like buttercups like a blonde whore's hair; alley by alley I will search and destroy like Code Six and Riley and I did in the old days.—Potato chip bags scuttered down Jones Street like the flittering red-brown places where "declassified" Army films had been censored; and Jimmy remembered Code Six in the days when he was a tanned, smoking, bare-chested soldier beside him unkinking a belt of 7.62 machine-gun slugs; he remembered the blue, blue mountains, the swarm of 'copters; and he could not believe that he was actually remembering anything because he had not done that since before he started drinking, and he felt uneasy.—In the marine gardens of the Tenderloin, he went beachcombing for special objects like the perfect pink shells of Peggy's ears. On the hood of Code Six's Lincoln, a whore very elegantly drank a Coke through a straw, a thin straw in which the liquid rose and fell as her tongue played with it, and the can seemed very precious in her fingers.—Pretty good, grinned Jimmy, feeling his old self. He wandered to the edge of Union Square where the department stores began (and Leroy and Laredo drove by him and Laredo said see, there's that old drunk again), and a pretty whore came after dark and sat on a bench looking with great interest at the pedestal and he wandered past the yellow-glowing snailshell dome of City Hall and turned the corner to the place where the blowjobs were; he revisited all the alleys with the wholesome names: Fern, Olive, Myrtle and Cedar which smelled of something other than cedar; and then—why, he had another drink.

A man walked crying down the street. He did not know that he was crying. He thought he was happy. So was he happy if he thought so? He was Jimmy with his wide owl eyes, his forehead wrinkled like a sandbar, his short grey hair like dying grass, his mouth gaping as he listened to someone talking or not talking to him, and his slender arms hung down at his sides.

An old woman stood on the sidewalk staring at him. He had never seen her before. She wore a raincoat much too large for her, and her wrists were so lost in the sleeves that they clutched each other for comfort. Her eyeglasses took up half her face; behind the smoked lenses, hard little seeds blinked and blinked. She seemed to be gathering breath as she fixed on him; she was glaring at him wildly, as if he had tried to murder her. In a moment she would start screaming. He looked around him for an alley to duck in, but there was none.

The woman began to weep.—Clark? she said very weakly. Clark, is it you? You came back?

Jimmy understood. His arm was around her.—Yeah, it's me, he said. And I came all the way to see you. I knew you were waiting for me. I felt it so I came. And you're looking good and looking happy. Now I'll always be here with you because even if you can't always see me I'll be right around the corner watching out for you and you can trust me on that because what I have in this bag gives me special powers. So don't you worry about ghosts and things like that because I'll be keeping my eye on you and I'll be helping you.

She clung to him. Her face was against his shoulder, and she was shaking. Her hand moved tenderly across his face. Supporting her, he led her to a doorway and sat her down.—I've got to go now, he said. But don't you ever worry anymore.

Everything's going to be grand.—He disengaged himself. When he looked back at her, she was smiling with closed eyes, sitting pale and still like a ruined doll.

Yessir! he shouted as soon as he had gone around the corner. I have the treasure.

No one paid him any attention.

He strode along kicking at sacks of garbage and whistling. He stuck his hand into the treasure-bag and winked. He dragged his knuckles across the bars of ground-floor windows. Then he saw that they were grime-black, and rubbed them on his pants. He sang don't letcher DEAL go-a *down*, ooh, whoo-whoo, till that last old DOLLAR is *gone!* and George the shoeshine man on Jones Street who was feeling poorly said my Lord Jimmy you sure are *cheerful* today and Jimmy said morning George and George said morning or afternoon either way sure is a nice day ain't it? and Jimmy said sure is, 'cause I got a SPECIAL THING in this paper bag and you can't even drink it!—George said well Jimmy whatever it is you get me one if it turns you around like that because I got *aches* and I got *pains*. Oh Jimmy old man you are a *card* do you know that?—Knew it all my life, said Jimmy. I'm such a card I shuffle when I walk!—And George stood laughing under his hat in the shade of his stand with all the little tins of Kiwi polish stacked beside bottles of this and that, and rusty shoehorns rattling like wind-chimes in the breeze, and boots hanging from hooks just over his head like the extremities of hanged men; and when Jimmy was gone George began to sweep the sidewalk chuckling.—Shucks, he said to himself. If that poor old coot got reason to be happy, I oughta have reason too. Ain't that right, boots? Happiness ain't against the law?

Cynthia

Cynthia leaned up against the door of a loading dock with her legs crossed. The sunlight glowed upon her right knee, her left flank. Whenever men passed by, she took a deep breath and thrust her chest out. She was smoking a cigarette, and her hands were tight little fists on her hips.

You want some company? Cynthia said.

His eyes went up the long sweep of Cynthia's legs, Cynthia so cool with a never to be lit cigarette in her hand, Cynthia tapping her shoes on the concrete, one fist on hip, the other firm against her shoulder as she leaned staring into his eyes with a fierceness that might have been predatory were the message not *feed on me . . . eat me . . .* and her gaze was not even fierce, really, but simply very serious because Cynthia was working and that was how she showed it. Then he thought to himself this is the one.

Yes said Jimmy I want you to fuck me with this wig on and hair all around your face like the rays of the sun and keep calling me your husband.

Whatever you say, laughed Cynthia. But you gotta pay me sixty right now.

Sixty bucks is too much, Jimmy said. I'm not asking to fuck you up the ass or anything.

All right, fifty then. I'm really good, said Cynthia. I run circles round them all. And you don't have to use a rubber or nothing. Now let's have the money. I be tired of playing around.

OK, Jimmy said.

Gimme gimme. Oh you husband.

Jimmy got it out of the lining of his coat, counting out the tens by feel, and passed it to her.

Now gimme the wig, Cynthia ordered.

When she had Gloria's crown of office in her hand, she started laughing and laughing cruelly. —Is *this* what she looks like? she screamed, puffing her lips out and smushing her mouth up against her nose, so that her nose and cheeks got fatter and her black eyeballs sparkled. Thunderstruck, Jimmy gaped at her; then he tried to snatch at the wig, but Cynthia leaped back and began to run down the street. Just before she vanished from his life for ever, he saw her throw the wig down into a sewer.

Budweiser

When Jimmy understood what had happened, the world seemed filled with sickness like liquid, churning him around in its acid waves, stinking in his nose and mouth, and he had to lie down on the sidewalk to stop it and felt better for a minute, but then he began to feel a hard remorseless oval in his belly, weighing down his guts as if he had swallowed a big lead sinker; this commenced to get burning hot so that he cried out and doubled his body tight, trying to squeeze that red-hot ball back into something soft and harmless, but he could not, and presently began to vomit very painfully on the sidewalk.

Home again

My god Jimmy cried Pearl what happened to you should I take you to a doctor?

Jimmy said hello Pearl here's my rent.

Cynthia

Cynthia started whoring when a friend said hey you're getting on your back for free you might as well make some MONEY at it!—The best thing that ever happened to her was when she got picked up by an army guy who had something wrong in the head. He gave her a bunch of fifty-dollar bills and said how much does it add up to? and Cynthia counted it and found that it came to a thousand dollars. The army guy said baby you just do whatever you feel like doing. She only had to stay with him a couple of hours. She spent it all on drugs.

Cynthia's man was in the pen. He'd be out in 1992. Until then, she wouldn't be kissing *nobody*. Whatever she did she had to do, but she was saving her kisses for him.

Jimmy

Pal you look very emancipated, said Code Six, meaning emaciated, and Jimmy said yes I am emancipated from my fatty flesh and Code Six shouted stop talking like a fucking *fag*! now get off your Gloria kick and eat right and Jimmy said look who's talking and Code Six said so I don't practice what I preach but that's no reason for you to cave in like me Jimmy boy you been the smart one you save your SSI checks so you always got a hotel room to stay in now don't end up like me stinking and puking in the alley I feel bad I ever encouraged you in this Gloria business because *look* what it's doing to you and Jimmy said Code Six we go back a long way but if you want to keep me as a friend don't try to break me up with Gloria ever again do you hear what I'm saying? and Code Six said that's how it is huh and Jimmy said yes and Code Six said hell James you know I didn't mean nothing.

Home again

Hello, Pearl, Jimmy said.

Pearl raised her upper lip and put lipstick on it. I've had it with you, she said. You never make any effort with me. Don't think I'm gonna give you any more breaks around here. Just pay your fucking rent.

Code Six

After Code Six had failed in his mission of persuading Jimmy to return to the paths of full-cocked righteousness, he ambled slowly home to Sixth Street. He did not like the Tenderloin because it was not his area. Bad things could happen to him here. Back home he could take care of himself. He crossed Market Street whistling sadly. For a week or so he'd been wearing a black eye. He didn't even remember who'd punched him. He now wandered in search of a pleasant corner, shrugging shamefaced as he looked people in the face who avoided looking back because he was Code Six whose greasy hair fell across the bridge of his nose, borne down by the weight of the filth it carried, Code Six with his stubbled wobbly chin that could still look pugnacious when he threw his head way, way back, Code Six with his great hairy jelly-belly that hung over his belt absorbing sunlight on this mild morning as Code Six took off his shirt and began to beat it like a carpet against the steel shutters of a hardware store—*whooh*, you *stink*! he shouted crossly at the shirt, at himself, and then he started laughing because no one would look him in the eye.—None of you stink as much as me! he shouted proudly. You can shit your pants all day and you still wouldn't bear a *candle* to me! Haw! Keep the flag flying high, streaming and flapping like thunder!

Viet Cong

Later, when he'd panhandled two dollars and was bombing along on the Night Train with such power and speed that the sidewalk was a blur beneath his tightrope feet so agilely lurching, he saw three Indochinese children sitting on the steps of a hotel, holding bundles of some grasslike herb in their hands. Each was chewing on one of the stalks, looking at him alertly. The little girl's blue-black hair was drawn back from her forehead by a headband. She sucked and sucked on her stalk, wrinkling her forehead. Her brothers stared at him unwinkingly.

Code Six cleared his throat. You know, I once *killed* slopes, he said haltingly. I was ordered to. But it made me feel real sorry.

The children looked at him. He ducked his head and hurried away.

As soon as he was around the corner he began punching himself.—Am I out of my fucking *mind* to be talking to SLANTS? he shouted into a Vietnamese market. Nobody looked at him.—Was I talking bullshit or batshit or dogshit or was it just ratshit? he said. Jeez oh jeez Jesus. I better stop hanging around James. He's wearing off on me. Goddamn.

Shit, he sighed. Every last *one* of us betrayed by the VC. Jimmy brainwashed, the Wrecking Crew all dropped dead, Riley God knows where, and me left to fend for myself here in the middle of motherfucking Hanoi, USA. Nothing to do, nothing to do. Wanna *kill* those Chinese Charlies! Come out and fight! he shouted.

Nobody came.

Guess I won that one, said Code Six, and he lay down on the sidewalk and went to sleep . . .

26

The Black Rose

It was another early morning afternoon at the Black Rose for Jimmy, when everything seemed quieter and slower— even the lights around the mirrors seemed to be blinking more slowly—and a slow snowstorm went on inside the pop-corn machine, with a rich smell of butter blowing across the bar in hot and oily waves, and two men sat at the end of the bar with their caps pulled down and an old man sat halfway to the bathroom with his head in his hands and a Budweiser in front of him, and Jimmy ordered a Budweiser and stared down at the old popcorn and dead beer bottles on the bar, and there were crumpled napkins with lipstick on them in the ashtrays and Jimmy's beer tasted like rotten hay.

Jimmy said have you seen Luna today? and Regina said making a face no I have NOT seen Luna and a couple of the Transformers begged her to turn on the stage lights (but not Phyllis because Phyllis was in jail) and so Regina flipped the switch and the Transformers started dancing to the music of the jukebox with the light-bubbles from the disco ball whiz-zing through them and Jimmy sat looking at a bottle behind the bar with a giant die on top of it and then Luna came in and all the Transformers yelled *Luna! Luna!* and Regina said well you asked for Luna there she is she'll manipulate you to *death* and Jimmy said politely I'm looking forward to it and Regina said if that's what you want and Luna danced and came and hugged Jimmy and she was wearing a wig that he had given her and she felt his pocket and saw that he had her sunglasses and said oh you kept them how sweet and Jimmy said yes I'll keep them forever unless of course you want them back and Luna said yes let me borrow them for fifteen minutes and Luna said now come home with me baby and we'll smoke a little pot together and Luna's dick was very big in the crotch of her leotard and Jimmy said OK but before Luna was ready he got restless again . . . These days he couldn't do any one thing.

In the park across the street it was hot and stinking, but finally a breeze came to liven up the flies, and pigeons showed up and pecked at stains, and a tired old woman in red sat cleaning her glasses with a dirty tissue. The earpieces hung limp, like the legs of some dying crustacean.

Code Six's Lincoln had finally been towed away.

Jimmy walked up the street to Geary and Jones and stood looking at the High Tide bar with its sign-lights spilling out of a neon cocktail glass. He stumbled and shook his head. Then he went back to the Black Rose and ordered another beer.

Jack and Dinah

There's the bastard, said Jack.

Beat his ass! shouted Dinah. Knock him down and give it to him!

Jimmy looked around thinking he was still in the Black Rose but he had somehow gotten to Hyde Street where he was all alone except for men leaning up against the walls and Jack hit him once lightly to knock him to the ground and Jimmy remembered as if it were just last night the time when he had had to defend all women from the fat boy at the dildo store on Turk and Larkin and he was strong from giving up Nicole for Gloria so that he lifted the fat boy easily a foot or two off the floor and punched him, but now for some reason he had no strength left as Jack knelt down on his chest looking both ways like a child about to cross the street before

126

he began to hit Jimmy in the face and for Jimmy it was as if
he were rocking and rattling with the motion of a train and
then Dinah was bending over him too and doing something
to him and something in Dinah's hand went click-click and
Dinah was doing something else to him and it was like being
in one of the little dark theaters on Larkin Street that he
used to go to where a whore would sit on his lap and ride
him up and down so that he rocked and rattled painfully
trying to look around her hair that smelled like phony straw-
berries and *hear* around her grunting breaths as she cut the
crotch of his jeans and Jack was saying come on come on
look at him he's pissed his pants but for Jimmy the screen in
that theater curved like the inside of a woman's breast and
the curtain swept aside showing a film about a train ride
which he thought at first was a Western the way the boxcars
rolled through the desert but then Louisiana began to flash
by and Jack said come *on* and Dinah said I have to get his
money now or I'll get vi'lent. I have to cut his wallet out of
him. I have to

Remembering the porno message

Later, a week later, when he came out of San Francisco
General with a pair of hand-me-downs and a bag lunch, it
was beginning to get dark as Jimmy walked down Ellis Street
scuffing his feet and kicking old newspapers and he saw a
black couple who smelled of innocence kissing in a doorway
so seriously and he thought how sad the way men can talk
to women with such calm deep love in their voices like steady
rivers and then they forget the beauty of the river like I did
he said to himself and now I can only hear it roaring all the
time in my ears like gravel of static; and he remembered how
once when he kicked the broken pay phone that he used to
call Gloria from, two dollars in quarters came spewing out

of it like puke and he used the money to call a lesbian porno message and the phone clicked and licked like a girl unsnapping her dress and Jimmy held his dick in his hand listening and the message moaned *Biting your tongue off* . . . but there was a bad connection and so after that Jimmy heard only a long crackle of static until finally he heard *a thousand people are* WATCHING . . . and then came more static and then Jimmy heard *I lift up your skirt, and you're kissing me and telling me:* SUCK ME, SUCK ME, SUCK ME . . . and then there came another crackle of static and Jimmy was frantic, thinking that he was missing all the best parts.

The Coral Sea

They called him Scarface now, like he was in the movies. Jimmy said well boys I was decorated in the service of my duty and they said yaah the Purple Pecker Award! and Jimmy leaned against the bar rocking and blinking stupidly. A guy said aw leave ole Gramps alone. At the Black Rose they said Jimmy's not the same anymore but at the Coral Sea they hadn't noticed anything so Jimmy liked the Coral Sea better.

Gloria

Then one day it came to him and he said well now if every-thing is upside down you can't have what you love if you have to have what you can't ever love if happy stories are sad then sad stories must be happy. That's all there's left to get: sad stories.

Candy

Jimmy got a beef stick and leaned up against a building chewing it and watching the whores. He saw one whom he had fucked and for a very long time he said to himself now what was her name? I remember how the cop called her Chrissy when he pulled her over but she was going by some other name oh hell what's it matter the names change almost as fast as the people around here. He saw a fat old whore standing between two cars, and every time a car slowed down or hinted in any way that it might be preparing to park she walked out into the street smiling with her hands on her hips. Jimmy watched her for about half an hour. He decided that he sort of liked her. Every couple of minutes she ducked down and checked her make-up in the side mirror of a parked car and then spread it like syrup upon the fat pancake of her face and Jimmy almost loved her because she was such a loser. Finally she decided to move to another corner and turned toward him and Jimmy said well how's it going and she said not bad you wanna date and Jimmy said sure and she said well I thought you was waiting for a bus or something and Jimmy said yeah you were so beautiful I was just standing watching you.

How much you wanna spend? the whore said practically.

I'll give you twenty dollars to take me up to your place and tell me some sad stories and then later I'll buy your panties off you you're just my wife's size she's been looking for a pair like yours not that I've seen them yet of course but I can tell you have good taste I know my wife will be very happy.

My name's Candy, she said. What's yours?

Jimmy.

Well Jimmy let me have the twenty right now 'cause I kind of owe a guy some money.

Here you go, said Jimmy, thinking shit well there goes that.

But she actually came back, smiling at him and saying see you can trust me I'm *people*.

I guess so, said Jimmy. He didn't really want to say much to her on the street. There were too many people around.

Now listen Jimmy said Candy I don't want to hurt your feelings or anything but I have to tell you what I tell all the elderly gentlemen: my time is VALUABLE so if you can't get it up I'm not gonna wait forever you see what I'm saying?

I can't do that anymore, said Jimmy. All I want's sad stories.

They started walking down to Turk Street, and Candy swung by an alley and looked in a paper bag behind a parking meter to see if her emergency stash was still there and it wasn't and Candy said shit and then Jimmy said shit because he saw the black-and-white rolling up. The cop talked to Candy for a while and Candy was loud and earnest, and then the cop motioned Jimmy over.

Jimmy pretended not to see.

C'mon, c'mon, Candy said. He wants to talk to you.

Well I'll *be*, said Jimmy. He ambled up to the black-and-white with mild surprise in his eyes.

Who are you, partner? the cop said, leaning on his hand and grinning.

Jimmy.

Where are you from?

Around here.

The cop looked at him in the eye for a long time. —Get back on the sidewalk, he said in disgust.

Candy laughed and laughed. You know what he said to me he said well I've heard the expression robbing the cradle but now seeing your date Candy I'm gonna coin a new one robbing the *grave*!

I'm so grave said Jimmy (keeping up the spirits of the world to the last) that sometimes I'm even serious.

You sure you can still get it up? said Candy anxiously. You look like you been through some rough times.

Candy and Jimmy went down to the Hotel Tony and stood outside the grating until a pimply-faced blonde came out and then Jimmy rattled the bars a little and she opened the door and said say do either of you have a dime for the phone why *hello* Candy! and then Candy pressed the buzzer on the inner door and there was a click and she pushed the door open and they were in the lobby of the world-famous Hotel Tony where Lonnie and Mason sat with arms folded behind the table and other men stood watching on the shabby stairs and Lonnie said three dollars to get in and Jimmy said with *pleasure* Lonnie and peeled three ones out of his wallet and Lonnie said thank you brother and Jimmy said how much to stay here for a week? and Lonnie laughed and said we only rent by the hour and Jimmy said aw come on and Lonnie said well since you're with Candy you must be all right you can stay for sixty-five a week and Jimmy said how many rooms can I rent at once and Lonnie said as many as you want and Jimmy said OK Lonnie I'll take a thousand rooms with maid service now where's the swimming pool how many goldfish swim in it? and Lonnie laughed heh heh heh and all the men on the stairs laughed and Candy said come on Jimmy we have work to do and Lonnie showed off his silver Liberty dime and his Indian head penny and Jimmy gave Lonnie a Canadian two-dollar bill and they both talked about rare coins laughing and laughing and trying to see who could say the stupidest things about old money and Mason and Lonnie passed a jug of Night Train back and forth and offered some to Jimmy but he said winking thanks anyhow fellas the lady says we have *work* to do and went upstairs with Candy to a room where Candy knocked and a woman said we're busy so Jimmy and Candy walked up and down the corridor three times and Candy knocked again and there was no answer and she said now when we come out there's gonna be someone waiting and you gotta give him five for the room and Jimmy didn't like that much but what could he do about it so Candy turned the knob and in they went. Candy bolted the door.

It was the usual kind of room with a double bed and stacks of *Playboy* and old record albums and the smell of incense, a punching bag over the bed, a pin-up of Farrah Fawcett, a refrigerator, and dozens of leather jackets hanging on the walls for quick conversion into cash for still other alchemical conversions whose results could at that very moment be heard out the window in the smash of a bottle against the sidewalk.

If anyone knocks on the door do *not* answer it, said Candy, going into the bathroom. She closed the door and was very quiet in there for a very long time and the TV said the Pope was careful when he praised Bolivia's efforts to curb the thriving drug trade and a bus went loudly by outside and Candy was quiet in the bathroom, shitting corncobs or shooting up probably as Jimmy had half-suspected she would be when he first saw her because she was dressed in a sweater and long pants as if she did not want to show any needle tracks (although later that night he saw her working in a black miniskirt) and children were laughing in the hall outside.

When at last she came out Jimmy said well now Candy tell me some stories. Sad stories. I need 'em sad so I can make 'em happy.

You meet a lot of different kinds people in this work, said Candy, staggering and wandering. Automatically, she started to strip. Her breasts were long and brown and covered with black sores. She stripped down to her panties and then remembered that Jimmy was not flatbacking her and stood confused for a second and then said well I wanna try on this skirt my sister gave me this is the kind of shit I wear, and she began to model herself for him, wiggling her fat paunch and shaking her tits from side to side and saying yeah lots of strange people out here.

That's for sure, yeah, said Jimmy noncommittally. He had already unzipped his pants.

132

You meet them psychos, you meet them people that like to be tied up, chained up, handcuffed from one end of the bed to the other and good god I'm talkin' about *torture* and you meet men that bring like them backpacks that have different equipment in 'em that they can hang shit from the ceilings. And they like to be hung up by their ankles and they like to be whipped.

That's right, said Jimmy with his dick in his hand, that's right.

Now me I'm a nice person and I lose a lot of money that way, because a person can look at me that way and tell that I'm not one of 'em. Some broads they can pull it off; I can't.

Is that a fact, said Jimmy, breathing hard.

The first time this guy wanted me to handcuff his arms to each side and his ankles were down here in some kinda thick rope but the rope was real soft, too. I'm talkin' 'bout the rope thing he wanted it so tight that you know when you take one of them ace bandages and wrap it around to cut off the circulation well it was too tight I said man your feet are gonna fall off but well he's into pain, you know. And I was scared at first. I ended up doin' it. He likes you to spit on him and when I spit on him he wanted me to take a safety pin and you seen them long safety pins, real thick, and he had one of them and it was unfolded out straight and what he wanted me to do is pull the skin back on his dick and the hole that's on it and he wants you to stick that safety pin down into the hole that's in his dickhead.

Is *that* right? laughed Jimmy, staring at Candy and choking as he jerked himself off.

Me I'm not no pain freak. I started out slow, and he gets mad 'cause I'm not doin' it hard enough and he's into *blood*. He got to arguin', and he got to callin' me names and shit an' *I* don't *like* to be called a bitch I don't care *who* you are if you call me a bitch you'll make me mad an' I will cuss you out an' I have come up and slapped people, so I guess he knew where most women's weak spot's at, and that's all it

133

took, so then when I got it in there I twisted it around, and you know I was doing it to be an asshole but he *liked* it, laughed Candy. He got different sizes of safety pins, so after you do that he likes you to take a safety pin and stick it through his nipple from one side to the other and then once it's on there he like for you to pull it back and forth like this and he locks it up, and when it's locked he likes for you to stick your fingers in and pull as hard as you can. Now, if *that* don't work, if you can't draw blood out with that one, he wants you to take your mouth and he wants you to bite it. That man, he's into blood real bad. And words kept goin' back and forth between us, 'cause I was too gentle. It seems like the more blood he'd see and the more madder he'd make me, the happier he was.

Jimmy came in his hand. *That's my dream!* he shouted.

Not so loud, said Candy. We don't want folks to think you're hurtin' me. Here's some toilet paper.

No, said Jimmy, *that's my dream you just told me*, when Gloria was trapped on the stairs by all the bad things she ever heard because you just told me all the bad things and now I know the two pimps got Gloria and raped her and cut her cunt out and now everything's all right. It's what had to happen. Oh, Candy. Oh, Candy, oh Candy Candy Candy. Now Gloria can never get away from me anymore. And it's not Peggy's dream anymore because you just made it mine.

Candy sat on the bed shaking her head slowly and thinking while the TV played music and Jimmy waited so expectantly and Candy said Gloria and Candy said *hmm!* and Candy said you meet all kinds in *this* job, I'll tell you.

Candy

Candy had learned many lessons in her life, the most important of which came when she was with a painting contractor who always carried a suitcase full of money when he met her and took her to a real nice hotel on Broadway and pulled out a bullwhip and sticks made of that wood called *whipping willow* and got out his cocaine and every time he got a register he wanted Candy to whip his ass until the blood came and then whip his back and whip it and whip it until Candy said well I have to go and the john said wait a minute and gave her more money and she whipped him for another forty-five minutes and then she said well I really have to go now and he gave her more money and then the light dawned on Candy: to get money she only had to threaten to leave, to become unavailable and therefore perfect like Gloria, and *then* she glowed with the light of a good thing coming to an end and easily achieved that perfection and they paid her and paid her.

Candy had also learned never to hurry a person, 'cause if she treated him with respect he just might come back.

Gloria

Now they were together forever and this time it *was* forever, and Jimmy said remember when we had that fight about our dreams and you came over for dinner at my place that time and I showed you my collection of clay people with razors stuck up their cunts and Gloria laughed and said yes darling I remember and I remember looking in the refrigerator and seeing that you weren't taking care of yourself and didn't have anything to eat that we hadn't just eaten so I got you a bag of groceries and Jimmy said I remember how you pissed in my mouth while Dinah stood clicking that stiletto I gave her and I remember the smell of your perfume as you sat beside me and how you were so interested in the clay people and even though you'd made half of them yourself back at the river with me and you looked at each one for such a long time and said things like I like the way this one's shaped or I like the face on this one and I felt that you were so interested and I gave you one of them and you kissed me and it was such a rich sweet kiss that I'll never forget it.

Let me kiss you again now, Gloria said. And then cut me again. Cut more of me out.

And Gloria was with him, and Jimmy was happy, almost completely happy; he was happier than he'd ever be again, and he kept thinking if only she was here too then it *would* be perfect; then it would be the three of us.

The end of the story

One night Riley hopped a freight into town, and because he had been living the life of himself he was in bad shape. He had been in Code Six's platoon. Pretty soon he found him on Sixth Street.

Well fucking *guy*! cried Code Six, delighted. (He stank worse than ever; his odor illuminated the darkness of the alley.) — I thought you was long buried and full of worms! — Pretty soon, said Riley. I got cirrhosis; liver's gonna pop any time now. — Well *die* like a soldier is all I say! Code Six exclaimed. You was always the bravest of us three, Riley — meaning, you, Jimmy and me — and I count on you to do honors to the fuckin' flag and keep it flyin' *high*! — How *is* old James? said Riley, and Code Six said you mean you never heard? and Riley said heard what? and Code Six said buy me a jug and I'll tell you all about it.

Well, said Code Six, I was down on Turk Street about eight years ago. No, about six years ago, actually. An' this was on check day, y'know, the day everybody gets their check. And there was some kinda *outburst* outside, by this restaurant. — Which restaurant? said Riley. — The Chink's, the Chink's, the Chink's! said Code Six, the chop suey house, you idiot. — Yeah, I *got* that, said Riley in a dry voice. — Yeah, fuckin' *slopes*! said Code Six, *slope* food! An' all the sudden I hear a *gunfire*! And I been in Nam just like you, and I know gunfire when I hear it, rather than a Polish Jew!* You know,

---

* This cynical name for a firecracker comes about, I presume, from German days, because when you set fire to one it leaves the world with a harmless bang, scarcely ever injuring its murderers.

gunfire has a distinct sound to it; once you hear it in a combat situation, no, you'll never forget it. And I look up, man I look around—I'm kinda jittery; only been back in the States about maybe ten or twenty years, still got that shit on my mind—I hear *gunfire*, and I know it. I turn around, man, and here comes Jimmy with his whore chasin' him! Usually were the other way around, weren't it? Damn! And she *drilled* his motherfuckin' ass, *good* and *proper*. Oh, man!—Code Six chuckled until poor Riley thought he must dissolve under the stench.—Jimmy comes in, the bitch comes in, just lit him up, right there! And she killed him dead right in front of the whole goddamned restaurant, and there were about twenty people in there, cooks and all—right bare-ass from my eyes! I said, *motherfucker*, I was safer back in Nippon, man, 'cause at least that way I know where the field of fire is! And that was how Jimmy died. Died like a hero. I never did find out what he had done. But *you* might 'a' knowed his ass, man. And might 'a' knowed *her*! It was old Gloria!

Damned right I knew Gloria, said Riley. I remember that chick. Fucked her once. God but she was free with her cunt. So she turned pro, huh? And she killed Jimmy, right on Turk Street?

That's right where he got lit up, man, right in front of the goddamned Ching's Chop Suey, whatever the fuck the name's of the Chink! Right next to Fred's, you know what I'm talkin' about. And I loved that bastard. He coulda saved the world. Lit him up, man, right in front of my eyes! And she knew her shit! She had some kinda training or somethin' like that. She knew how to kill. She had a .38. She didn't miss 'im. She come *blazin'*, and *blood was blastin'*, and the Chinamen were fuckin' splittin'! You know how a mother-fuckin' *slope* is, man!

Glossary

The following list of terms is for the reader who may not have constant access to whores and drugs. (Some of these words, of course, are location-specific, such as "black-and-white"; police cars are differently colored in different areas.)

Assing—Tricking.
Black-and-white—Police car.
Box—Vagina.
Company—Sex.
Date—Trick.
Decepticon—A perfect transvestite.
Fix—Addict's required dose of drug (usually injected).
Flatbacking—Missionary position intercourse.
Golden shower—Sex act in which one partner urinates on the other.
Half-and-half—Fellatio followed by straight intercourse.
He-she—Transvestite.
Ho *or* **hole**—Prostitute, or sometimes simply a woman.
Hubba—Cocaine processed into smokeable "crack".
John—A prostitute's trick.
Love—Sex.
Miss Thing—Transvestite.
Shit—Anything you shoot into your arm.
Smack—Heroin.
Smoke—Hubba.
Snitch—Police informant.
Speedball—Heroin and cocaine.
Transformer—Transvestite.
Trick pad—Hotel where the prostitute brings her tricks. (She usually lives elsewhere.)

Ten/two—Old term for sex in a **trick pad** ($10 for a **flat-back** + $2 to get into trick pad). A more accurate term now would be forty/five.

A Profile of the Tenderloin
street prostitute (1985-1988)

If it pleases you to collect generalizations as some collect postage stamps, then this little whore's album may be of interest to you. Of course that folly of statisticians, the composite person, does not exist. Nonetheless, many of the street prostitutes whom I have met in the Tenderloin share important similarities, which I list below. — But before we get to them, the following points: (i) I have always assumed that the prostitutes who answered my questions told the truth (ii) it would most likely be very foolish to apply this profile to other groups of prostitutes, such as call girls or senators. Nor would the street prostitutes of even ten years ago necessarily match those described here. The current deadly plague of sexual disease has probably made streetwalking a more desperate and dangerous activity than it used to be, with concomitant natural selection of its practitioners (iii) this profile does not begin to address the issue of whether or not the prostitute is a victim, whether her relationship with her clients is particularly exploitative to one party or the other, etc. However, one conclusion is apparent from the facts presented. *The unpleasantnesses of her profession are largely caused by the criminal ambiance in which the prostitute must conduct it.*

The points below apply to prostitutes who are women. There is an addendum on transvestite prostitutes.

1. The prostitute offers sex without commitment.

- **White prostitute, early 30s:** The street's a pretty scary place, but a lot of them are just normal men who

141

want a blowjob before they go to work, a piece of ass, just got in an argument with their wife, it's their revengeful trip, you know. As long as they use a rubber, it's cool. Don't bring your wife home nothin'. I was married for a great deal [of] years; I respect that. When I married my husband, I asked him if he had any desire to stray. And he said I'm looking, I can't deny that I'm looking, I'm noticing other women. I said just make sure she's a prostitute, 'cause I know she'll give you back. And it worked. We had like five six happy years together after that. Alcoholism's what broke it up.

2. In general, she does not enjoy the work for its own sake

• **White prostitute, early 30s:** I run into a real lot of nice guys, but, you know, it's an automatic shutdown. Like when he got out of the pen it took me a day not to shut myself down with him, 'cause I hadn't been with him for so long. He took it pretty offensive. All I could tell him was hey I'm sorry. But that's what it's about. We just shut ourselves down, an' do what we know.

3. However, she does appreciate the money, which can be phenomenal

• **Black prostitute, mid 20s:** When I was working in an office, it didn't matter how whether I was sick for a day or whether I worked an extra day. I always knew exactly how much I'd make at the end of the week. I couldn't stand it. Out here I can make as much as I want to make.

• **White prostitute, mid 30s:** I once made $7,000 from a single trick. And it was nothing fancy, either.

4. **She is well aware of the risks of disease, and usually insists that her johns use a rubber**

• **White prostitute, early 30s:** As far as I'm concerned, as long as you're clean about it, and you always take the precautions of a rubber, there's nothing wrong with it, 'cause the only thing *I've* ever made love to out here's a rubber.

• **Black prostitute, early 20s:** I always use a condom, and I check 'em; if their penis looks raggedy, if it looks like they have an infection or it leaks, all money isn't good money. I won't go with them.

5. **She is or has been a junky.***

• **White prostitute, early 30s:** It fills the emptiness.

6. **Her johns, particularly drug dealers, often prefer to pay her in crack. It is cheaper for them, and they know that they exercise more control over her by dangling a fix in front of her. She is well aware of this.**

• **Black pusher, late 20s:** You want to get your dick wet? Don't *never* give her no money! Give her a little smoke, and then start walking away from her. She'll do whatever you want to do. I ain't never paid for pussy yet, and I ain't never used a rubber.

• **Black prostitute, mid 20s:** There's a lot of girls out here that do things just for rocks. That's not something I believe in . . . because then you're just trading yourself for a drug. I don't smoke cocaine. I have, but not much.

---

* Younger prostitutes tend to be crack users; older ones are intravenous drug users.

7. **She was usually introduced to prostitution by a girlfriend already in the profession.**

• **Black prostitute, late 20s:** My first date was in 1981. My girlfriend said you want to know how to get some money? I'd rather get paid than do it for free. When I got money I said this is cool.

8. **Her career progressed so gradually that the first trick was no particular milestone.**

• **Black prostitute, late 20s:** Supposedly you'd be fired [from the massage parlor] if they caught you fucking, but everybody did it. I didn't at first. But then I found out I could get $5 more for jerking them off a little, $10 more for taking off my top, $20 more for taking off my bottom, so I kept doing a little more and a little more ...

• **Black prostitute, late teens:** I'd always been fucking around. Why not get money for it?

• **White prostitute, mid 30s:** First I just gave blowjobs. I never had to take down my pants. Then I gradually started flatbacking.

• **Black prostitute, mid 20s:** Q. Who was your first one?
A. I don't even remember.

9. **She sets limits to protect her privacy and her sense of self.**

• **Black prostitute, mid 20s:** I won't never kiss anyone except my son's father, and he's in jail in Arizona. He'll be getting out in 1991; then I'm gonna marry him.

● **White prostitute, early 30s:** I won't let men abuse me or call me bitch no matter how much they pay.

● **White prostitute, late teens:** You can call me Suzy; that's my trick name.* Don't matter what my real name is.

● **White prostitute, early 30s:** An Oriental no I don't want to call him Oriental I'm sure he's an A-rab of some sort picked me up once and wanted to go to the hot tubs and he kept talking about how he really wants to be in me and how he wants to eat my pussy and really be involved and well that's not what we're about here. We don't *make love* to our dates. We *service* them. We make ourselves available for them to go ahead and get inside. Well he got me so shook about he couldn't be rushed he needed a lot of time he was pretty detailed what he wanted to do with my body an' I got the impression he wanted to crawl right up inside me so just before we got to the hot tub I said look I'm sorry but I don't think I can accommodate you. I knew I could get away with saying that 'cause I'm real soft spoken I have a real good upbringing I was married for thirteen years.

10. **Being a professional, she takes pride in her skill, either to satisfy her johns or else to "process" them quickly and efficiently.**

● **White prostitute, early 30s:** But it's my *choice* to give a man pleasure, 'cause I'm real *good* at it. Most of 'em are married and they need a different taste of woman.

---

* *Note*: Trick names often fall into one of three categories: (1) words associated with pleasure (Joy, Felicia, etc.) (2) words associated with luxurious things than the john can eat or drink up (Candy, Brandi, etc.) (3) names that sound "aristocratic" or "fancy" (Stella, Melissa, etc.).

● **White prostitute, early 20s:** I lie there and spread 'em; I give 'im twenty minutes. End of that time, either he leaves or he pays me *more money.* You see, *I* know how to do it!

11. **For the same reason she likes to claim that she, not her johns, is in charge. But she more often expresses fear than confidence.**

● **White prostitute, mid 30s:** You know, a woman in here is really in control. It's really up to us. [*But a few seconds later she said:*] If they pull a knife on us all we can do is talk our way out of it.

12. **She has a list of safety rules for herself to follow.**

● **Black prostitute, early 30s:** You have to be a good judge of character, for one. I won't go somewhere where I'm not familiarized. If someone wants me to go to their house, I get half an advance at least, at least a hundred dollars depending on whether they're close. I let someone always know where I'm going. I make 'em show me a driver's license.

13. **However, she will break the rules if they prove inconvenient.**

● **White prostitute, mid 30s:** I don't usually date black men but it was pretty hot out policewise and so I made an exception. Black guy drives up in a nice car, looks pretty proper, he's got a briefcase in the back seat. That's what we check for—what kinda business he might be in. And another thing I don't like is anybody taking me past Market Street. That's too far out of the territory. I allowed him to do that.

14. She has been raped by a trick once or twice.

● **White prostitute, early 30s:** I never dated black people, 'cause I always heard that black people were the ones that would go off on the prostitute. — Bull*shit.* — I've had two bad experiences, an' it's been by white men. And what was so killing about it was it's been by older white men.

First one was in '81, his name was John, and he was 47 years old. Big old *fat* sonofabitch. He was in a pickup truck with a gas station uniform on. He told me that he wanted a blowjob for twenty-five dollars in the truck; I said cool. And at that time we was usin' this parkin' lot around the corner here, an' when we got to the corner I says turn, turn; he didn't turn. He stepped on the gas; he went through every light from Turk Street down to the other side of Market. People keep on saying well how come you didn't jump out? Motherfucker you think I'm crazy you think I'm gonna jump out as fast as he was goin'? Mmm-*mmm*. So when we finally go to where he was goin' he did what he pulled a gun out and held it up to my head. From 7:30 to 10:00 that night he had me fuck him suck him. He dropped me off on Broadway at that restaurant Clown Alley and when I got out I was cryin' and cryin'. Some man picked me up I told him what had happened and stuff, so he ended up giving me a hundred and sixty dollars *an'* takin' me home.

Two weeks later a guy in a Volkswagen came up to me. I don't know how he knew *my* name. Anyway he says Sandy where's your girlfriend Candy? And at the time I *was* hanging around with a girl named Candy. I says well she's at home. He says well you wanna go instead? I says well what's up? He says I tell you what I do he says I take five pictures and I pay seventy-five dollars. An' I says cool. I got into the Volkswagen, and I'm telling him what happened to me with the man with the gun an' he's giving me all thus bullshit an' he's oh that's a goddamned shame they oughtta stiffen the laws on people like that. Well OK, so we finally parked; he reaches down in between the driver's seat and the door; next thing you know, *click!* there came a big old fucking knife. It happened so fast! I say you lousy motherfucker! A knife I'll talk shit, but a gun . . . well, I can't outrun a bullet, OK? And all he wanted me to do was suck nice and I said you can get your dick sucked; just don't hurt me, OK? Just don't hurt me. He says I'm not gonna hurtcha. So we had a discussion. Why you tell me about Candy and stuff? And what happened, Candy burned him. He was into cocaine. You know, half these tricks that come down here are into cocaine, OK? They want to front the girl their money and then they're gonna get their cocaine and shit like this. Half the time they end up getting burned, so what the john does, he ends up picking up somebody else, you know with dark hair or blonde hair or whatever's similar to her, and ends up taking it out on *her* . . . I just happened to have dark hair and long legs.

15. She has also been robbed or attacked by people other than her tricks.

• **White prostitute, early 30s:** I been jumped out here, 'cause like I said my male was in the pen. I didn't have anybody representing me. My man is not a pimp, but everybody knows when a woman's out on the streets alone. I had six guys jump me for my money, so I was robbed once. I've had two jealous women jump on me, one because of another guy that I dated—I didn't know that that was the one *she* was tryin' to pursue and date— my other one was a big fat black chick out here, who's

148

robbed every woman there is out here because she can't get a date, so she takes our money.

16. She takes going to jail from time to time as a matter of course.

• **Black prostitute, early 30s:** Like the first night I did it I went to jail. And that would become a pattern. Every time I came to a new town, I'd go to jail the first night. Then after that, I'd make MONEY ... The Vice will always bust a new girl, one that don't know what they look like.

• **Black prostitute, early 30s:** What happened was, Japanese guy got me a case, thirty dollars for a blowjob, and so then he told me he was a cop, and no problem; I don't ever give 'em no hassle or anything, because it *is* a misdemeanor and I *will* be released. So, just go through the preliminaries of going down there and getting booked and then getting cited out. When you're in jail it's just girls. They only talk about shit that's on the streets, what they wanna do when they get out; if they're new to jail they wanna make themselves seem like they're hot shit.

17. She may support a man on their earnings. (He too frequently has a drug habit.) She buys him clothes, a car, etc. She loves him, but often feels exploited.

• **White prostitute, early 30s:** You know, up to now I've never given a man the space for a relationship, due to the nature of my job, 'cause what they want is the money I'm capable of making. I never really chose a man until last year. Then I did and I got quite hurt by it, I just really loved him. He was no pimp, mind you.

Never tried to pimp me. But it doesn't hurt him to take my money. I had a real nice bank account waitin' for him when he got out, bought him a car, and he started an argument about does my name need to be on the registration of the car? I feel that it should, since it's my money that paid for it, but he wants it all his. OK, so I let that go. He gave me a beautiful jade necklace, beautiful. Took that back last night. Just told me he wanted it back. So I gave it back to him. And I found out he pawned it today. And that *crushed* me. It's really difficult. We had a relationship before I ever came up here, but he knows how to take advantage of it.

18. Her man can be abusive.

● **Black pimp, late 20s:** Some of those girls you just have to politely hit 'em upside the head. One minute they want you to love 'em; the next they want you to abuse 'em. I think they're confused.

19. He can also protect and assist her.

● **Black prostitute, early 30s:** I don't worry when I hop in the car 'cause my man he take down the license plate number.

● **Black pimp, early 30s:** Oh listen man am *I* glad to see you. She's in jail. I need forty-five dollars to get her bail and I've gotten most of it but I'm still fifteen short. Can you help me out? I swear to you, man, I'll give it back to you on Saturday.

20. She remembers a happy childhood.

● **Black prostitute, early 30s:** I was a very happy little girl. We did lots of fun things. I remember going to Knott's Berry Farm, stuff like that.

21. She also remembers playing sex games, and feeling slightly guilty about them.

● **Black prostitute, late 20s:** One of the things I remember as a kid was the first time I played doctor with the little kids, somewhere between three and five. I think I was about four. And this little girl that I used to play with and her older brother, they got me, and I was playing with them in a garage in the back of their house. I remember being on the table. It seems there was something draped over the table and I was on the table. [*Laughs.*] Had my clothes off, I'm sure. They had a bottle of fingernail polish, and he was paintin' my privates. It seemed fun at the time. I remember knowing there was something wrong and not wanting my mother to know I had fingernail polish down there. I remember he later got mumps on the bottom of his feet, and they moved away.

22. She distrusts most or all the other street prostitutes, but remembers a Golden Age when they all helped each other.

● **White prostitute, late 20s:** I remember the days when all the girls tugged on each other's coat tails to warn you if the Vice was coming. All that changed when the black girls started coming in from Oakland. They and their pimps would rob you and jump you soon as look at you. I don't trust anybody now.

23. She is pessimistic about her future.

● **White prostitute, early 30s:** Q. So what things do you think are going to happen to you in the future?

A. If I don't get out of this I'll have to go back to bartending. And that's not really that good of an option.

Q. How long do you think you can do this?
A. Not too much longer. I'm gettin' real tired from it. Real tired. [*Long pause.*]

NOTE ON THE TRANVESTITE PROSTITUTE

Not all the above points apply to this lady. She often does enjoy the work for its own sake, and sometimes volunteers her companionship gratis. She is less cautious about disease. She is, in fact, less cautious generally, since she has a man's body and a man's strength to even the odds a little against those who seek to prey on her. (Many transvestite prostitutes have also been raped, however.) She less often sets limits with her clients; she rarely supports anyone else, and she seems much more optimistic about her future. She is less often a drug addict.

Street Prices for Hair, Sex and Other Things (1985-1988)

Commodity	Price Range
Kiss	Free-$5
Lock of hair	$10-$20[1]
Hand job	$15-$25
Blowjob	$15-$25
Modeling for porno photographs	$15-$25
Flatback	$40-$50[2]
Golden shower	$40-$100
Ass fuck	$60-$75
Double date	$80-$100
Lesbian sex	$100-$200
S & M: whipping the trick, etc.	$100-$300 or more
S & M: being whipped by the trick	$200-$500 or more
S & M: piercing, stabbing the trick, etc.	$300-$500 or more
S & M: being pierced, stabbed by the trick	?

---

[1] More generous portions provided if wig hair.

[2] To put this in perspective, consider the following: a massage parlor prostitute usually charges $30 for the massage, plus $70 to $100 or more as a "tip" for flatbacking. A call girl charges $50 for the outcall (which goes to the agency), plus at least $100 for the flatback. Higher priced call girls can command considerably more.

Extras

Rubber	Free (prostitute carries)
Entry into trick pad	$3-$5
Use of hotel room in trick pad	$10-$15

For scholars only

Interviews	Free or 50¢-$1/minute
Portrait photographs	Free or $3-$5/photo